"I'd like to take you to bed for the entire weekend,"

Jamison told Blythe with a gleam in his eye.

"At least you're honest about your intentions," she said in a strangled voice.

"I didn't make myself clear. That's what I'd *like* to do, but I'm not going to."

"I don't understand. What's wrong with me?"

"Not a thing that I've been able to discover. You're the kind of woman men marry. I don't think you make love lightly," he answered gently.

"What's wrong with that?" she asked defensively.

"Nothing, but you deserve someone equally committed. Unfortunately, I'm not that man."

"Aren't you jumping to conclusions? We've known each other exactly a day and a half. I don't want to marry you. I like my life fine just the way it is."

He smiled. "Then we don't have any problem."

Dear Reader,

What a fabulous lineup we have this month at Silhouette Romance. We've got so many treats in store for you that it's hard to know where to begin! Let's start with our WRITTEN IN THE STARS selection. Each month in 1992, we're proud to present a Silhouette Romance novel that focuses on the hero and his astrological sign. This month we're featuring the charming, handsome Libra man in Tracy Sinclair's *Anything But Marriage*.

Making his appearance this month is another one of our FABULOUS FATHERS. This delightful new series celebrates the hero as father, and the hero of Toni Collins's *Letters from Home* is a very special father, indeed.

To round out the month, we have warm, wonderful love stories from Pepper Adams, Geeta Kingsley, Vivian Leiber, and as an added treat, we have Silhouette Romance's first PREMIERE author, Patricia Thayer. PREMIERE is a Silhouette special event to showcase bright, new talent.

In the months to come, watch for Silhouette Romance novels by many more of your favorite authors, including Diana Palmer, Annette Broadrick and Marie Ferrarella.

The Silhouette Romance authors and editors love to hear from readers, and we'd especially love to hear from *you*.

Happy reading from all of us at Silhouette!

Valerie Susan Hayward
Senior Editor

ANYTHING BUT MARRIAGE
Tracy Sinclair

Silhouette
R O M A N C E™
Published by Silhouette Books New York
America's Publisher of Contemporary Romance

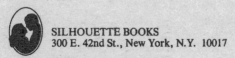

SILHOUETTE BOOKS
300 E. 42nd St., New York, N.Y. 10017

ANYTHING BUT MARRIAGE

Copyright © 1992 by Tracy Sinclair

LOVE AND THE LIBRA MAN
Copyright © 1992 by Harlequin Enterprises B.V.

ISBN: 0-373-08892-2

First Silhouette Books printing October 1992

All the characters in this book have no existence outside the imagination of the author and have no relation whatsoever to anyone bearing the same name or names. They are not even distantly inspired by any individual known or unknown to the author, and all incidents are pure invention.

®: Trademark used under license and registered in the United States Patent and Trademark Office and in other countries.

Printed in the U.S.A.

Books by Tracy Sinclair

Silhouette Romance

Paradise Island #39
Holiday in Jamaica #123
Flight to Romance #174
Stars in Her Eyes #244
Catch a Rising Star #345
Love Is Forever #459
Anything But Marriage #892

Silhouette Special Edition

Never Give Your Heart #12
Mixed Blessing #34
Designed for Love #52
Castles in the Air #68
Fair Exchange #105
Winter of Love #140
The Tangled Web #153
The Harvest Is Love #183
Pride's Folly #208
Intrigue in Venice #232
A Love So Tender #249
Dream Girl #287

Preview of Paradise #309
Forgive and Forget #355
Mandrego #386
No Room for Doubt #421
More Precious than Jewels #453
Champagne for Breakfast #481
Proof Positive #493
Sky High #512
King of Hearts #531
Miss Robinson Crusoe #565
Willing Partners #584
Golden Adventure #605
The Girl Most Likely To #619
A Change of Place #672
The Man She Married #701
If the Truth Be Told #725
Dreamboat of the Western World #746

Silhouette Books

Silhouette Christmas Stories 1986
"Under the Mistletoe"

TRACY SINCLAIR,

author of more than thirty Silhouette novels, is a Scorpio. "I'm not sure if I really believe in astrology," the author says, "but I sure seem to fit the Scorpio profile!" An extensive traveler, this California resident has accumulated countless fascinating experiences, settings and acquaintances to draw on in plotting her romances. "I especially enjoyed the opportunity to write about two Libras," Tracy says. "Libras are a lot of fun—everyone likes a Libra!"

LIBRA

Seventh sign of the Zodiac
September 23 to October 22
Symbol: Scales
Planet: Venus
Element: Air
Stone: Opal
Color: Blue
Metal: Copper
Flower: Calendula
Lucky Day: Friday
Countries: Japan, Argentina, Austria
Cities: Lisbon, Vienna, Antwerp

Famous Libras

Dwight Eisenhower
John Lennon
Mahatma Gandhi
Charlton Heston

Eleanor Roosevelt
Margaret Thatcher
Martina Navratilova
Barbara Walters

Chapter One

Blythe Reynolds was drawn to the large abstract painting in the gallery window from the moment she saw it. The vivid colors were what first caught her eye, but when she stopped for a longer look, the bright splashes began to take form. Indistinct shapes in the center of the canvas resembled a pair of scales—the sign of Libra, *her* sign. Clearly she had to have that painting.

She went inside, trying to decide whether to hang it in the living room or the bedroom, where she actually spent more time. After a saleswoman told her the price, she didn't have to make a decision.

"I had no idea it would be that much," Blythe said regretfully.

"Gustave Grabowski is making quite a name for himself. His works are a good investment," the saleslady assured her.

"I'm not a collector, I just like the painting. But I hadn't planned to spend that much.'"

"We might be able to arrange a payment plan. Are you visiting in San Francisco?"

"No, I work a couple of blocks from here," Blythe said. "I'm a copywriter at Harmon, Wiley & Trent."

"In that case, I'm sure financing would be no problem."

"Let me think about it," Blythe answered evasively.

"Certainly." The woman handed her a card. "I'm Lydia Cartwright, and I'll be happy to help you if you decide."

Blythe's mind was already made up. Her budget didn't allow for such a wild extravagance. Although she made a good salary at the ad agency, there was never much left over at the end of the month. She left the shop with a wistful feeling of regret.

The painting remained in the gallery window for weeks, in spite of the artist's supposed popularity. Blythe got in the habit of stopping to look at it every day on her way to or from work. It was almost as good as owning it—and a lot cheaper.

But one day that wasn't enough to satisfy Blythe. Her alarm clock had failed to ring and she was late for work. Then the ad campaign she was working on was scrapped, meaning she'd have to start over from scratch. The last straw came at the end of the day when the senior partner informed her that her request for a raise had been turned down, even though she'd been promised one weeks ago.

Blythe's green eyes were smoldering as she jerked on her coat and stalked out of the office. It wasn't fair! She felt overworked and unappreciated.

Even "her" painting didn't lift her spirits. She stood outside the gallery staring moodily at the vivid abstract. What was the point in working like a mule when you didn't even get a pat on the back? Rebellion suddenly overwhelmed her. She deserved a reward for all she'd put up with.

Marching into the gallery, Blythe said to the saleslady, "I'd like to buy the Grabowski you have in the window."

"You looked at it a couple of weeks ago, didn't you?" Lydia Cartwright asked. "I'm so glad you decided to take it. I think you'll be happy with your choice."

"It's going to put a serious dent in my budget, but I decided, what the heck." Blythe shrugged.

"This isn't an extravagance. You're really making a wise investment."

The woman removed the painting from the window and took it to her desk. As she was opening her salesbook, they were joined by another saleslady.

"What are you doing with the Grabowski?" she asked.

"This customer just bought it," Lydia told her.

"That's impossible! I sold it yesterday."

"It doesn't have a red tag on it."

"I guess I forgot to put one on, but it's definitely sold. The gentleman gave me a deposit. He's going to be here after work today to pick it up."

Blythe wasn't about to accept that, especially after the day she'd gone through. She set her chin pugnaciously. "It wasn't marked sold, so you have an obligation to sell it to me."

"I'm dreadfully sorry, but he gave me a deposit."

"What if he changes his mind? I'm prepared to give you a check right this minute." Blythe had come to regard the canvas as her own, and she didn't intend to give it up.

The three women were so deep in their argument that they didn't notice the man who had entered the gallery. He waited for a few moments with thinly veiled impatience.

After glancing a couple of times at the thin gold watch on his wrist, he finally said, "Excuse me, but could one of you help me? I've come to pick up my painting. I'm Jamison Marshall."

"Oh, Mr. Marshall, I'm so glad you're here," his sales-lady said. "There's been a bit of a mix-up. This woman wants to buy your Grabowski."

Jamison's expression held male appreciation as he looked at Blythe's wide green eyes, creamy skin and shining auburn hair. His discreet gaze also took note of her slender figure and long, shapely legs.

In spite of the favorable appraisal, he said, "That's unfortunate. Perhaps you have another one of his works you can sell her."

"I don't want another one!" Blythe exclaimed. "I want this one."

"So do I, and I saw it first."

His response was unexpected. Men were usually anxious to please her. She took a more calculated look at him. Under different circumstances, Jamison Marshall would have won her unqualified approval. He was in his middle thirties, tall, athletically built and extremely handsome. She'd always liked the combination of dark hair and blue eyes. That wasn't the only attraction, however; his face had character. Those pronounced cheekbones and square jaw indicated determination—even ruthlessness if the occasion demanded it. This man was used to getting what he wanted.

Blythe knew instinctively that arguing would only make him more adamant, so she took a different tack. Adopting a soft, appealing manner, she said, "This painting means a lot to me. I'd really appreciate it if you'd let me have it."

He looked amused, as though seeing through her act. "Why does it mean so much to you?"

"Because I'm a Libra," she explained eagerly. "You see those shadowy shapes in the middle? I'm sure those are meant to be scales. That makes it very personal to me. It's almost like a sign from heaven."

"Someone up there is playing a little joke on you, because I'm a Libra, too," he said calmly.

She looked at him uncertainly. "You're just saying that."

"Nope, I was born on October fourteenth. When's your birthday?"

"October third," she answered in a muted voice.

"So we're even on that score, but I'm still one up on you. I put down a deposit yesterday."

"But you didn't actually take possession, and I was here today ahead of you." Blythe fought the losing battle valiantly.

"I happen to be an attorney, and I'll give you some free advice. That argument will never stand up in court."

"You'd sue me?" she gasped.

He grinned. "Why not? I wouldn't have to hire a lawyer."

Blythe had to concede defeat. He did have a prior claim, and nothing was going to sway him. She mustered a tiny smile. "I guess you win. I hope you enjoy your painting."

His amusement vanished as he gazed at her dejected face. "You're really disappointed, aren't you?"

"Terribly!" She answered, hope returning. "Are you sure you won't change your mind? I'll give you visitation rights," she joked.

He stared at her thoughtfully. "That might be the solution. Perhaps we should share the painting."

"How could we do that?"

"We can split the purchase price and each keep the picture for three months at a time."

"You can't be serious! We're total strangers."

"What difference does that make?"

"A lot. I don't know anything about you."

"I could say the same about you, but I'm more trusting. Are you worried that I'll abscond with your half?" he asked dryly.

"It's possible. You could be a very clever con man."

Instead of being insulted, he laughed. "We're not talking about a Picasso. Don't you think you're being unduly suspicious?"

"Not necessarily." She eyed him narrowly. "Why would you make such an offer when you don't need to?"

"I happen to be a very generous fellow. I was trying to do something nice, but if you're not interested we'll forget about the whole thing." He turned to the salesladies. Both women had been listening avidly. "I'll give you my check for the balance due."

"Wait!" Blythe couldn't let her painting slip away. His plan might be unconventional, but it had one definite advantage. She'd only have to come up with half the money. "I didn't say I wasn't interested."

"Does that mean you've decided to accept my offer?"

She hesitated. "I'd have to know more about you."

"That's understandable. Well, let's see. You already know my name. I'm thirty-four, in excellent health, I'm reasonably good at sports and I enjoy the theater and all kinds of ethnic foods. Except maybe Greek. I'm not overly fond of having to dig through wet leaves for my dinner."

"I wasn't inquiring about your personal life," Blythe said primly, although she hadn't stopped his recital.

"You want some assurance that I'm a solid citizen? I can see my profession doesn't count." His eyes sparkled with laughter. "Will my banks and club affiliations do?" He brought out a wallet stuffed with identification and membership cards in numerous organizations.

She was impressed. Jamison Marshall was everything he claimed to be. His address on Nob Hill was among the finest in the city, and the clubs he belonged to were noted for being exclusive. She began to feel slightly foolish.

"Do I pass the test?" he asked.

"I suppose so," she said uncomfortably.

"Now may I ask *you* a question?" A little smile played around his firm mouth.

"I'm not in your economic bracket, but I have an excellent job," she answered defensively before he could quiz her. "You don't have to worry about *my* absconding with the painting, either."

"I'm not worried, and that wasn't my question. I was merely going to ask your name, since I take it we have a deal."

"Oh. It's Blythe Reynolds." She looked at him uncertainly. "Don't you want to know any more than that?"

"I suppose I should know your address and phone number. I'll write mine down for you, too."

After they'd exchanged slips of paper, Blythe asked, "How are we going to decide who gets it first?"

"Flip a coin?" When she nodded, Jamison produced a quarter. He tossed it in the air, then covered it with his hand. "You get to call."

"Heads," she said.

He uncovered the coin and showed it to her. "Too bad. You lose."

"Oh well, three months isn't the end of the world. At least I'll have something to look forward to."

He stared appraisingly at her delicate face, his gaze lingering on her soft mouth. "I can't believe that will be the high point in your year."

"Maybe not, but I've been looking at this painting every day for weeks. I never actually thought I'd own it."

"Perhaps you should take it first," he said slowly.

"No, you won fair and square. We have to abide by the rules for this thing to work." Blythe was rummaging through her purse with increasing anxiety. Finally she uttered a cry of dismay. "Oh, no! I was in such a hurry this morning that I forgot my checkbook."

"No problem. I'll pay the full amount, and you can give me your half later."

"I'll go right home and get my checkbook," she promised. "I'll bring the money to your house."

"There's no hurry," he assured her.

"I'd feel better about it. Besides—" she flashed him a pixie smile "—I don't want you to change your mind once you get our painting home and see how fantastic it looks on the wall."

"I never promise a lady anything I'm not prepared to deliver, but I'd be delighted to have you come over for a drink."

A doorman took Blythe's car when she drove up in front of Jamison's imposing apartment house. The lobby was furnished like a living room, with a damask-covered sofa and down-filled chairs. A glass coffee table sitting on an Oriental rug held a large arrangement of fresh flowers. If the lobby was this elegant, she couldn't wait to see Jamison's apartment.

It didn't disappoint her. The elevator opened onto a private, marble-floored foyer with double doors. Beyond them was an entry hall that led to the largest living room she'd ever seen. It was exquisitely furnished, but Blythe couldn't take her eyes off the view. Floor-to-ceiling glass windows gave a panoramic sweep of the city that was breathtaking.

The Golden Gate Bridge predominated, arching over blue water filled with sailboats and a distant freighter chugging into port. In another direction were the tall spires of churches and a cluster of modern skyscrapers.

"It's magnificent," Blythe exclaimed, unable to look away.

"Yes, San Francisco is a beautiful city," Jamison agreed. "Shall we have our drinks outside?"

She'd been too dazzled to notice the terrace, another surprise. It was almost as large as the patio of a private home. Enclosed by a low concrete wall with wrought-iron guard rails, the paved expanse held garden furniture and big planters filled with trees and flowers.

"Who would think there was an honest-to-goodness garden on top of this building?" Blythe marveled. "Where are the swimming pool and tennis court? On the other side?"

"That would be ostentatious." He smiled. "What can I fix you to drink?"

"I'll bet if I asked for something exotic, you'd have all the ingredients."

"Probably not. Contrary to what you think, I don't have everything."

He beckoned her to follow, and led the way to a paneled den next to the living room. Two walls were lined with bookshelves flanking a built-in bar. The soft music that filtered through the apartment came from an elaborate stereo system housed in another wall.

Blythe glanced around. "About the only thing I can see that you're missing is a wife. Do you have one of those, too?"

"No, I don't."

His rather grim tone of voice made her wonder. Had he been married once and had a bad experience? His sudden reserve warned her not to ask questions. Not that she would have. Theirs was a business relationship, nothing more.

"I'll write you a check while you're bartending." Blythe paused as she opened her purse. "But if you're in a hurry, please say so. I don't have to stay for a drink."

"You'd be doing me a favor," he answered graciously. "I have the entire evening free."

She was sure it was by choice. Even without his obvious wealth, Jamison was a fascinating man. She stared at him covertly as he took an ice tray from the under-the-counter refrigerator and filled a silver ice bucket. He'd changed from the elegant suit he'd worn at the gallery into equally elegant fawn-colored slacks, a white silk shirt and a cream-colored cashmere pullover. The casual outfit emphasized his broad shoulders and lean hips. No doubt about it—he was a magnificent male animal. Blythe hurriedly opened her checkbook.

He didn't want to take her money at first. "Wait until it's your turn to have custody. It isn't fair for you to pay for something you're not getting for three months. You can give me a check when the time comes."

"No, Jamison," she said firmly. "We have a deal."

"Call me Jamie. Jamison sounds so stuffy. Nobody but my parents calls me that."

"All right...Jamie. But you really must take the money. I'd be very uncomfortable otherwise."

"You really *are* afraid I'll change my mind, aren't you?" he teased.

"No, I just like to pay my debts. Where do you plan to hang the painting?"

"I hadn't really thought about it. Where would you suggest?"

Blythe frowned thoughtfully. "It would get too much competition from the view in the living room. You wouldn't get to enjoy it as much, either. If you're like me, you spend more time in the bedroom."

He smothered a smile. "Some nights more than others."

Her cheeks turned pink as she realized he might think she was coming on to him. "I only meant I don't have your fantastic view, so I don't sit in the living room much. Except when I entertain, of course. But I don't do that very often." She stumbled to a halt, aware that she was babbling.

"Entertaining at home is getting to be a lost art," he agreed, pretending not to notice her embarrassment. "Perhaps because San Francisco has so many great restaurants."

"That must be it," she said, grateful for his tact.

"Shall we take our drinks outside?" he suggested.

The patio was scented by orange and lemon blossoms that covered the dwarf trees in large ceramic pots. Placed among them at intervals along the wall were round aggregate planters filled with flowering plants. Lobelia, primroses and many other varieties blended together to form a rainbow of colors.

While Blythe was inspecting the garden, Jamie lit a fire in a black metal brazier containing logs. The dancing flames were a visual delight and also provided warmth.

"This is charming." She held out her hands to the fire. "All we need are a box of marshmallows and a couple of long pointed sticks."

"Do you think marshmallows go with Scotch?"

"Not really. You don't seem like the outdoor type anyway."

"I wouldn't say that," he protested. "I'm very fond of sports."

"I was referring to the kind of man who likes to cook over a fire and camp in the woods in a sleeping bag."

"You're right, that's not my speed. Man wasn't meant to be zipped into a pouch like a kangaroo."

"Do you have claustrophobia?"

"No, I just like freedom to move around when I go to bed."

Blythe suspected he had more than his sleeping habits in mind. Jamie was undoubtedly an experienced lover, capable of arousing his partner to the heights, then satisfying her completely with that long, hard body. She glanced away hastily.

"Do I sense disapproval?" He chuckled.

"Certainly not," she answered primly. "Everyone is entitled to choose his own...uh...form of activity."

"Don't tell me you're a camper. You don't look the part."

"Appearances are deceiving. I'll bet I still know how to put up a tent. My parents used to take my sister and me camping when we were kids. What did you do in the summer?"

"Various things. Is your sister older or younger than you?"

"Claire is four years older, but we're very close. We talk on the phone almost every day."

"It's nice that you have such a good relationship," Jamie commented.

"The best. How about you? Do you have sisters or brothers?"

"I have one sister who lives in London."

"That's too bad," Blythe said. "I'd hate to be that far away from Claire. Do your parents live here, at least?"

"Occasionally. They both travel a lot." He gestured toward her glass. "Can I freshen your drink?"

"No, thanks, I really must be going."

"You can't leave yet. We haven't decided where to hang our painting. Do you have a date?"

"Well, no, but I thought you might have something to do."

"Nothing more interesting than what I'm doing now." He smiled charmingly. "Why don't we have another drink and then go out to dinner?"

"It's so beautiful here that I hate to leave," she said frankly. "Couldn't we send out for pizza instead?"

He looked at her with a puzzled frown. "You'd really prefer that?"

"Definitely." She grinned. "You look startled. Don't the women you know eat pizza?"

"I couldn't say. The subject never came up."

"Why doesn't that surprise me?" she murmured. "It's all right, we can go out if you'd rather."

"I wouldn't. Pizza sound like a great idea. Who do I call?"

"You poor man." Blythe shook her head. "Your education has been sadly neglected."

"I'm willing to learn." The firelight gave his laughing eyes an added glow. "And maybe in exchange, I can teach *you* a few things."

She felt a creeping warmth in her midsection when she thought about the things he could teach her. Blythe knew her experience wasn't even remotely equal to his. The realization sounded a warning in her brain. Was Jamie deceptively urbane? Surely it was her imagination, but suddenly he resembled a large, sleek tiger toying with its prey.

"Let's take care of *your* education first," she said tartly. "Where do you keep your telephone book?"

After Jamie had ordered, following Blythe's instructions, he hung up the receiver and said, "Okay, that's taken care of. Now we can get down to business. Let's go into the bedroom."

"Why?" She looked at him warily.

"Didn't you say the painting should go in there?"

"Oh." She was beginning to wonder if Jamie led her into these little traps deliberately, although his expression was innocent. "It was only a suggestion. You can hang it anywhere you please. It's your apartment."

"But I value your opinion. After all, we have a lot in common. We're both Libras."

"Do you think that's why we both fell in love with the painting?" she asked. "Did you see the scales in the center, too?"

"That's the interesting thing about an abstract," he answered evasively. "You discover new things every time you look at it."

Jamie's bedroom was as dramatic as the rest of the apartment. Similar floor-to-ceiling windows gave a different view, and the Golden Gate Bridge seemed even closer from here. The stream of tiny lights flowing over it in both directions looked like loose diamonds rolling in a straight line.

"This won't do, either," Blythe declared. "Don't you have any rooms without a view?"

"It isn't a real problem. I don't spend all my time looking out the window," he said mildly.

"I don't see how you can pay attention to anything else."

"I manage," he murmured, gazing at the cloud of auburn hair framing her lovely face.

Blythe was unaware of his admiration. She was glancing around at the king-size bed, the comfortable chairs and tables. There was even a marble fireplace on one wall.

"You certainly have everything any man could want in here," she remarked.

"Only if he was a very *old* man." He smiled.

She looked at him squarely. "You have to stop reading double meanings into everything I say. I'm not trying to be seductive. Maybe your girlfriends play those sort of games, but I don't."

He didn't try to deny her accusations. "I'm sorry. I was only teasing you. You're so delightfully innocent."

Blythe wasn't thrilled at being called innocent, even though that was essentially true. She didn't want him to make a pass at her, but no woman liked an attractive man to dismiss her as an ingenue.

Lifting her chin, she said vaguely, "I've known my share of men."

His eyes were brimming with laughter. "Are you speaking in a Biblical sense?"

"That's none of your business," she snapped.

"You're right, of course. It isn't. I wouldn't welcome questions about *my* personal life."

"I'll bet the answers couldn't be printed in a family newspaper," she muttered, stalking past him down the hall.

Fortunately the doorbell provided a diversion. When Jamie answered it, a doorman was standing in the entry holding a large white cardboard box with the name of the pizza parlor written in big red letters.

"A young man said you ordered this, Mr. Marshall." His tone indicated there must have been a mistake.

"Excellent, our dinner is here." Jamie took the box from him. "Thanks, George."

Blythe's amusement dispelled her irritation. "He looked so shocked," she said after the man had left. "Maybe we should have told them to deliver it in a plain brown wrapper."

Jamie inhaled appreciatively. "The garlic would have given us away."

"Let's just hope he doesn't tell the other tenants. Your social standing would be destroyed."

"That wouldn't worry me unduly." He led the way to the kitchen.

It was the only room she'd seen that wasn't spectacular. The kitchen was modern and had all the requisite appliances, but the walnut cabinets and white counters and floor were strictly utilitarian. A small square table and two chairs were placed by a window, but Blythe was sure Jamie had never eaten there.

He opened the box and gazed inside with a bemused expression. "Look. It's already cut in wedges."

"Amazing." She grinned.

"It isn't nice to make fun of people who haven't had your advantages," he said reprovingly.

"If pizza is all you've missed in life, it's hard to feel sorry for you," she replied dryly. "Do you know where the plates and napkins are kept, or should I rummage around?"

"You act as though I'm completely helpless," he said in an injured tone.

"That doesn't answer my question." She opened cupboards and drawers at random until she found the necessities.

When she carried them to the kitchen table, Jamie asked, "Wouldn't you prefer to eat in the dining room?"

"This is more convenient."

He looked vaguely dissatisfied. "I'm not entertaining you very royally."

"There's no reason why you should. This isn't a date. We're merely business partners."

"I hope we'll get to be more than that," he remarked as he seated her. When she glanced up quickly, his expression was bland. "I hope we'll become friends."

They lingered over dinner, talking and laughing as if they were already well acquainted. Blythe told him about her work at the ad agency and her occasional frustrations.

"It's rather ironic that I decided to buy the Grabowski because I *didn't* get a raise," she said ruefully. "That wouldn't make sense to most people."

"Why not, since it made you happy? Sometimes you have to follow your instincts."

"My horoscope this morning did say I should stop vacillating and make a decision."

"Well, there you are." He smiled. "It was written in the stars."

"I get the feeling that you don't believe in astrology," she said skeptically.

"If I didn't before, I'm fast becoming a convert." His voice was like deep velvet.

Blythe changed the subject. "Tell me about *your* work. What kind of a lawyer are you?"

"A good one, I hope," he joked.

"I'm sure of that, but I meant, what kind of cases do you handle? Criminal? Corporate?"

"A lot of my practice is devoted to divorce cases, unfortunately."

She grinned. "It's a dirty job, but somebody has to do it."

"I suppose so. A great deal of unpleasantness could be avoided, however, if people would simply live together."

"You don't believe in marriage?"

"From all I've seen, it doesn't work," he answered tersely.

"You scarcely get an unbiased picture. You only see people whose marriages are in trouble. How about all the couples who live long, happy lives together?"

"They might continue to live together, but that doesn't necessarily mean they're happy. People stay in rotten marriages for a variety of reasons."

"That's a cynical thing to say," Blythe protested. "I know a lot of very devoted couples."

"Possibly you only think you do. The doting behavior they display in public is often discarded like false eyelashes when they get home."

"Are you implying that women are always to blame for a bad marriage?" she asked indignantly.

"Not at all. Men are equally guilty. And neither of them ever learns. I'm handling a third divorce for one client."

"Those cases are the exception," she insisted.

"I don't agree," he maintained stubbornly.

"So your answer is to abolish marriage? How about the couples who really want to make a commitment to each other?"

"They don't need a piece of paper for that. If they truly love each other, they'll stay together. But if they fall out of love, isn't it better to part without bitterness and recriminations?''

"The affairs you're advocating don't necessarily end with a smile and a champagne toast to a lot of fun evenings," she answered tartly. "When two people break up it's bound to be traumatic, whether their relationship is legal or not. You have to take a chance. No one gives you a guarantee."

"Precisely. So why bother to go through the formalities?"

"You're implying that *no* relationship is lasting?" she asked slowly. "Don't you believe in love?"

"I think it has a better chance of enduring if some judge doesn't tell you that you *have* to spend the rest of your lives together."

"It's a good thing your parents didn't feel the way you do," Blythe said wryly. "Children need some stability in their lives. Or do you believe they should be abolished, also?"

Jamie's intensity faded, and he sat back in his chair, smiling. "Obviously my theory isn't perfect. I'm still working on the solution to that problem."

"I think you need to get into another branch of law."

"We can't all be Perry Mason," he said lightly. "I *was* offered a rather offbeat case recently, though. A couple wanted to sue a preschool nursery for expelling their four-year-old."

"You said it was offered to you. Didn't you take the case?"

"No, I referred them to one of my partners. The kid brought a hair clipper to school and shaved the other tots' heads during nap time. I couldn't have presented an effective plea, because my sympathies were with the nursery school."

"I must tell my sister about that." Blythe laughed. "Her four-year-old is an angel by comparison. Although she did spray the dog with Claire's best perfume. He'd rolled on the grass after the gardener had fertilized it.''

"At least she meant well."

They talked about things they'd done as children and how their parents had reacted. The time passed so pleasantly that Blythe gasped when she happened to glance at her watch.

"I had no idea it was so late! I have to go."

"It was a fun evening, even if we didn't get around to doing what we wanted to." He held up both hands hastily. "I meant, hang the picture."

"I knew that." She grinned.

"You'll just have to come back again," he remarked as he walked her to the entry. "How about tomorrow night?"

"I can't," she said regretfully. "I have to work late."

"That's too bad." He didn't suggest another night.

Blythe had to admit she was disappointed. Jamie was a fascinating man. Would he ask her out again? she wondered on the drive home. The prognosis wasn't good. He undoubtedly had a little black book filled with women's names. It could take weeks for him to work his way down to the Rs. Blythe's mouth curved mockingly as she remembered something. At least she could count on seeing Jamie every three months.

Chapter Two

The telephone was ringing as Blythe opened the door to her apartment. When she ran to answer it, her sister's voice greeted her.

"I know you weren't asleep, because I've been calling all evening and you were out," Claire said.

"I just this minute got in," Blythe answered.

"Where were you, and who were you with?"

Blythe laughed. "You're worse than Mother. At least she leads up to those questions subtly."

"Why waste time? We always tell each other everything."

"Wait till you hear what happened tonight." Blythe kicked off her shoes and curled up on the couch while she related the events of the evening.

"Wow! It looks like you really hooked a live one this time," Claire exclaimed.

"Not really. He gave up without a struggle when I told him I couldn't make it tomorrow night."

"That doesn't mean anything. He'll call you."

"I'm not counting on it. A man like Jamie can afford to be independent."

"I suppose you're right," Claire conceded reluctantly. "Young, rich and single makes him a natural target for predatory females."

"He has a lot more than that going for him. You've never seen eyes that blue or a physique that rugged. He's built like one of those Greek statues of Olympic athletes—broad shoulders tapering down to slim hips and long legs."

"That's usually evident because they're nude," Claire observed dryly.

"Claire! What are you implying?"

"Not a thing," her sister said hurriedly.

"I hope not. Jamie was a perfect gentleman."

"Too bad." Claire laughed. "Maybe he'll mend his ways."

"You're incorrigible," Blythe said disgustedly. "I was perfectly happy with the way the evening went."

"That's your whole trouble. You never want to get involved."

"I haven't met anyone who interested me longer than a couple of months." Blythe sighed unconsciously.

"Maybe this one will have more staying power."

"He's pretty special," Blythe admitted.

"Then don't let him get away," Claire urged. "If you don't hear from him within a reasonable time, *call* him. Women don't languish by the telephone any longer, waiting for a man to make the first move."

"I'm sure women call him constantly. The phone rang several times while we were out on the terrace, but he said the answering machine would take a message. He probably guessed who the calls were from."

"The important thing is, he didn't want to leave you for *anyone*. Don't sell yourself short, Sis, you're pretty spectacular yourself."

"You couldn't be prejudiced, could you?" Blythe asked fondly.

"No way. You're the beauty in the family. But it's time you picked out one lucky guy and settled down."

"If that's what you have in mind, you chose the wrong candidate. Jamie doesn't believe in marriage."

"What man does?" Claire chuckled. "But a smart women can convince him that he's dying to tie the knot. He'll even wind up thinking it was his idea."

"Not Jamie. I've never seen a man so violently opposed to the institution. It's because of his work. He handles all those messy divorce cases."

"Pastry chefs don't get turned off of dessert," Claire replied crisply. "Just assure him that marriage isn't necessarily a terminal disease."

"I don't want to get married, either. And if I did, I wouldn't want a groom I had to coax down the aisle."

"With an attitude like that, you're apt to wind up an old maid," Claire warned.

Blythe grinned. "At least I can count on having a date in my sunset years. Jamie and I will totter along on our canes when we go out to dinner."

"Someday you'll fall in love, and then you won't be so flip about marriage," Claire said direly.

"And you'll be waiting to say 'I told you so,'" Blythe teased. "But you'll have to defer the rest of your lecture. I need my sleep. Tomorrow's a workday."

Jamie didn't call the next day, or the one after. Blythe had given up hope when the phone rang on Saturday morning.

"What are you doing?" he asked.

"I *was* sleeping," she answered pointedly.

"It's too nice a day for that. How would you like to go sailing on the bay?"

Blythe briefly considered playing hard to get, then discarded the idea. She did express slight displeasure, however. "You might have given me some advance notice."

"I thought I was going to be tied up today. How about it? Will you go with me?"

That meant she was probably his second choice. The knowledge didn't delight her, but she wasn't annoyed enough to turn him down.

"Give me a little time to get dressed. I'm still in bed."

After a moment's pause he said, "I'm beginning to think *you're* the one who says suggestive things on purpose. I'm getting a vivid mental picture."

"Don't get carried away," she answered crisply. "I'm wearing a nightgown."

"I didn't doubt it for a moment."

"Is that so unusual? Most women wear nightgowns in bed."

He chuckled richly. "If you say so."

His meaning was all too clear. Jamie's women didn't wear anything when they spent the night with him. Blythe's imagination supplied the details. His blue eyes would sparkle like sapphires as he aroused his partner with drugging kisses and seductive caresses the length of her body. He would explore every erogenous zone with mind-spinning male expertise until she twisted in ecstasy, begging for completion.

"Are you giving me the silent treatment?" Jamie's voice dispelled the erotic fantasy.

"No!" she said breathlessly. "I was just...uh... wondering how much time I had to get ready."

"Tell me how much you need."

"At least an hour."

"You've got it. I'll see you soon."

Blythe raced around getting dressed in record time. She used a minimum of makeup and brushed her long auburn hair until it shone, then pulled on a sweatshirt and jeans. Not the glamorous outfit she could have wished, but suitable for the occasion. When the doorbell rang promptly one hour later, she was ready and waiting.

Jamie's gaze roamed over her with approval. "I see you're an experienced sailor. You'd be amazed at some of the getups women wear to go out on a boat. Would you believe high heels and earrings?"

"No, I wouldn't. Common sense should tell them better than that. But I don't want to mislead you. I don't have any experience."

"I'll be glad to supply it," he teased.

"On a boat," she said reprovingly.

"I'll teach you that, too."

"You'll teach me that, period," she answered primly.

He grinned. "Okay, if you want to be a spoilsport."

His mischievous openness allowed her to relax with him. She enjoyed his admiration and knew he would never become difficult. A man like Jamie didn't have to pressure a woman.

His boat was docked at the St. Francis Yacht Club on the marina facing the bay. They had breakfast at a table by the window, overlooking sailboats with furled masts bobbing in the water.

Jamie was well-known, and people kept stopping at their table. One was a handsome older man dressed in yachting clothes rather than the jeans and a windbreaker most of the other members wore. His white flannels were immaculate, and his navy jacket had a crest on one pocket.

"Jamison, my boy, I was hoping I'd run into you," he said. "I saw the countess in the south of France last week. She looked simply marvelous."

"She always does," Jamie answered before introducing the man as Harley Ainsworth.

When the amenities were concluded, Harley continued where he'd left off. "Sylvia sent her love and said you should call her. She'll be at the Ritz in Paris for a month."

"Thanks for telling me," Jamie answered with a slightly sardonic expression.

"Where is Freddy these days?" Harley asked. "I haven't seen him around in ages."

"Last I heard, he was in New York," Jamie replied.

"Probably hiding out until the ballet season ends here, if I know Freddy." Harley laughed.

"Perhaps. Ballet isn't one of his passions."

Jamie was polite, but Blythe sensed that he didn't care much for Harley or the people he was talking about. The older man didn't seem to notice his lack of enthusiasm. He continued on about the house party he'd attended, dropping titled names and bits of gossip that only he relished. His recital was interrupted when the waiter brought their check.

Jamie seized the opportunity. "It was nice running into you, Harley, but you'll have to excuse us. Blythe and I are going sailing."

"Have fun," the other man said. "And don't forget to call your mother."

As Blythe and Jamie walked outside onto the dock she said, "I didn't realize he was talking about your parents. They're in Europe?"

"My mother is," he answered briefly.

He climbed over the side of a sleek sailboat tied up to the wharf, then held out his hand to help Blythe aboard. She wasn't sure if he was avoiding the subject of his parents or if he was just anxious to get started.

Once they glided out onto the bay, Blythe had other things to interest her. It was a beautiful day, with a brisk wind that sent them slicing through the blue water at an exhilarating pace. But the wind also whipped Blythe's long hair around her face annoyingly.

When Jamie noticed her struggling with it, he brought out a yachting cap and tucked the flyaway strands inside. "It's a shame to hide this beautiful hair, but you'll be more comfortable," he said.

"Yes, this is much better." She was very conscious of his strong fingers brushing her skin.

He framed her face in his palms and stared at her critically. "You look flushed. Maybe I should put some zinc ointment on your nose so you don't get sunburned."

"I'll look like a clown," she objected.

"An adorable one." He smiled down at her.

His azure eyes were fringed with black lashes much too long for a man. They didn't detract from his virility, though. Nothing could. He had the taut body and imperious face of a pirate of old.

Blythe had further evidence of Jamie's masculinity when a wave slapped the side of the boat. She was thrown off balance, into his arms. He braced himself, supporting her weight as she tried to regain her balance. In that brief moment she was made unmistakably aware of his hard chest and the strong muscles in his rigid thighs. Her body retained the impression long after she was able to right herself.

"Are you okay?" He kept his hands on her arms to steady her.

"I'm fine," she said breathlessly. "That wave just took me by surprise."

"It was the wake of a motorboat. They're supposed to keep their distance, but hot-rodders aren't confined to the roads."

"Well, no harm done," she said brightly.

"I rather enjoyed it. Shall I look for another motor-boat?" he teased. "Or can we do a repeat on our own?"

"Isn't it a little public for that sort of thing?" she asked lightly.

"You're right. I don't like an audience."

"I'm glad to hear you're not an exhibitionist."

"No way. I give one-woman performances." He traced the shape of her mouth with a long forefinger.

Blythe knew Jamie was only joking, but for one fleeting moment she didn't want him to be. Which was utterly crazy! He was practically a stranger, and she didn't indulge in casual affairs.

"There's a time and place for everything," she said briskly. "And this isn't either one."

White teeth gleamed in his tanned face. "Does that mean I have something to look forward to?"

"That depends on what you consider an event," she replied calmly.

"You're a delight." He kissed the tip of her nose. "We're going to have a lot of fun together."

The wind was perfect for sailing, but it was getting cool by the time they returned to the wharf in the late afternoon. Blythe was glad when Jamie put the top up on his Corvette.

"What would you like to do now?" he asked as he got behind the wheel.

"I should go home and wash my hair," she answered. "It's a mess."

"I like it this way." He combed his fingers through the tangled strands. "You look natural and wholesome."

"That's a rotten thing to tell a woman," she said wryly.

"Dear heart, how can I please you? You get angry when I say I'd like to make love to you."

"You never said that!"

"I'm sure you know it. What man wouldn't want to? You have an exquisite face and the body of a siren." His eyes moved over her in an appreciative appraisal. "I'd like to take you to bed for the entire weekend."

"At least you're honest about your intentions," she said in a strangled voice.

"I didn't make myself clear. That's what I'd *like* to do, but I'm not going to."

Blythe felt as though someone had doused her with a pail of cold water. "I don't understand. What's wrong with me?"

"Not a thing that I've been able to discover." He smiled. "That's what makes it even harder."

"That's a lot of double-talk. Tell me the truth." She was too annoyed to let well enough alone.

He sighed. "Dear little Blythe. You're the kind of a woman men marry."

"You think I'd expect you to marry me if we—" She came to an abrupt stop.

"Let's just say, I don't think you make love lightly," he answered gently.

"Well, no, I...what's wrong with that?" she asked defensively.

"Nothing at all. It's very admirable. You deserve someone who will be equally committed. Unfortunately I'm not that man."

"Aren't you jumping to conclusions? We're known each other exactly a day and a half."

"I know my feelings on the subject."

"What I meant was, I don't want to marry you, either," she said angrily. "Or anyone else. I like my life fine just the way it is."

"Then we don't have any problem." He smiled.

"Except for your colossal ego," she fumed.

"I'm sorry if I hurt your feelings. You're a lovely, desirable woman."

"Don't patronize me," she snapped.

"It's true, and if I've offended you, I want to make up for it."

"Why?" she asked bluntly. "Our paths crossed by accident, so why not leave it at that, since our relationship isn't going anywhere?"

Blythe dimly realized that her anger was irrational. Jamie's reasons for not wanting to sleep with her were rather flattering, especially in light of his obvious attraction to her. But she couldn't help feeling rejected.

"I was hoping we could be friends," he said placatingly. "Relationships built on friendships are often the most rewarding kind. Don't you have any male acquaintances that you aren't interested in romantically?"

"Yes," she answered grudgingly.

The ones that sprang to mind were Doug Ransome, the head of the art department at work, and Larry Kramer, who was almost like a brother. She and Larry had gone all through school together.

"Do you enjoy being with them?" Jamie asked.

"Very much."

"Does it detract from the enjoyment because you know they aren't going to make a pass?"

"No, it's more of a relief. Especially after a date with an octopus who thinks he's irresistible." She smiled unwillingly. "I see your point."

"Then you'll continue to go out with me?"

"Why not?" Her good humor was restored. "A girl can't have too many friends."

That was the start of an exciting time in Blythe's life. Jamie took her to expensive restaurants and to the theater, where they always had the best seats. Those were the dates he made ahead of time, but he didn't always give her advance notice. Sometimes he would pop into her office at noon to take her to lunch. Or he'd phone unexpectedly in the evening and suggest a neighborhood movie. She never knew what to anticipate, only that it would be fun.

But there were other days and nights when she didn't hear from him. Periods when she suspected he was with other women—the ones he had a different relationship with. That was to be expected. Jamie was a sophisticated man, not a schoolboy.

Blythe tried not to dwell on his private life. The vivid pictures her imagination conjured up made her vaguely unhappy, foolish though it might be. She was having the time of her life. What more could she ask for?

One night when Jamie came to pick her up, he seemed preoccupied. During dinner Blythe mentioned the fact, since he wasn't his usual self.

"Is something wrong, Jamie? Your mind seems to be somewhere else."

"How could it be when I'm with you?" he asked fondly.

"You don't have to keep up a front if something's bothering you. Would it help to talk about it?"

He sighed, giving up the pretense. "I'm always a little bemused after I talk to my mother. She phoned just before I left to pick you up."

"Is she back from Europe? You could have broken our date if you wanted to see her. I would have understood."

"You're very sweet, but she isn't in town. She phoned from Greece to say she's going on a cruise."

"Your parents certainly lead a glamorous life."

He hesitated for a moment before saying, "Yes, I suppose you could call it that."

"Don't you? Your mother was at a house party with a countess not long ago, and now she and your father are going cruising in the Aegean."

"That's only partially correct." Jamie's mouth curved sardonically. "*She's* going, he isn't. My parents are divorced."

"Oh ... I'm sorry."

"Don't be. They're happier than they've ever been."

A lot of things about Jamie's outlook began to make sense. "Was the divorce recent?" Blythe asked in a muted voice.

"No, they finalized it when I was in high school and Angela was in college. But they'd grown apart years before. I often wonder if they were ever happy together."

"They had two children," Blythe protested. "They must have loved each other."

"Perhaps you're right. I never saw it, though. Their love died long ago."

"At least they were there for you when you were growing up." She didn't know what else to say.

"Not really. Angela and I went to boarding school in the winter and camp in the summer. When Mother wasn't traveling, she was busy with her social activities. And Dad was engaged in his own pursuits." Jamie's voice was derisive.

Blythe was appalled. The description of his family life was completely foreign to her. She'd read about the antics of the jet set, but they'd sounded like fiction. Her own family was close-knit and warmly supportive.

"Well, maybe it was for the best, then," she said lamely. "At least for them."

"It was. They're quite good friends. Dad even sent Mother a wedding present when she married the count," Jamie said mockingly.

Blythe's mouth dropped open. "Your mother is the countess that man was talking about at the yacht club that day?"

"She still uses the title, although the marriage was brief." After a look at Blythe's dazed face he said, "You can understand why I never told you anything about my parents."

"There was no reason why you should," she murmured.

"Let's get out of here and go dancing," he said abruptly.

Blythe felt constrained with Jamie for the first time. She ached with pity, which was the last thing he wanted. Fortunately the disco they went to was crowded and noisy. It wasn't meant for conversation.

Jamie seemed to work out his frustrations on the dance floor. When the music switched to a quieter beat, he drew Blythe close and rested his cheek on her temple. They moved together like one person, filling her with a deep contentment.

"This is nice," he murmured. "Just what I needed."

She tilted her head to look up at him. "I'm glad you're starting to relax."

"I apologize for being such a dull date tonight," he said ruefully. "I don't usually let my emotions get out of hand."

"You mustn't feel that way. You don't have to be superman with me. We're friends, remember?"

"I keep reminding myself of that constantly," he muttered.

Jamie usually said good-night at the door of Blythe's apartment, and that evening was no exception. He lowered his head and kissed her, which was also customary. It was always a token kiss, an expression of friendship. This time started out no differently. Blythe raised her face expectantly, and Jamie's lips brushed hers. But after a moment he reached for her, and the passion of his mouth increased. While his hands moved restlessly over her back, he deepened the kiss.

Blythe was drawn into a vortex of swirling emotions. His mouth was a flame she couldn't resist, and his lithe body was compellingly seductive. After a first, instinctive recoil, she didn't try to resist. But when she put her arms around his neck, uttering a tiny sound of pleasure, Jamie's embrace loosened.

Burying his face in her soft hair, he muttered, "I must be out of my mind."

Blythe clung to him for a moment until her emotions were under control. "It's all right, Jamie. I understand."

"I wish I did." He put her away gently and stared into her emerald eyes. "As you can tell, I'm not myself tonight."

She gave him a tentative smile. "That's okay. I like you, whoever you are."

His hands tightened on her shoulders for an instant, then his intense expression changed. "Good night, Blythe. I enjoyed the evening."

After he left, Blythe got undressed, but she couldn't fall asleep. The tumultuous episode in Jamie's arms had left her keyed up and unfulfilled.

She understood the reason for his behavior. The unhappy relationship with his parents was intensified by his mother's phone call, and he'd reached out for affection. Things had simply gotten a little out of hand. Blythe wished, a trifle wistfully, that he didn't regret it so much. She was happy to have been there when he needed her.

Blythe was prepared to tell Jamie that, but he didn't call for the next several days. That was unusual. Generally he called to say hello, even if they weren't going to see each other. She would have phoned *him*, but she decided he needed some time alone.

Toward the end of the week, Blythe was passing by the art gallery when Lydia, the saleswoman, called to her.

"I hope we're going to see you tonight," she said.

Blythe looked at her blankly. "What's happening tonight?"

"Didn't you get your invitation? We're having a showing of Grabowski's newest paintings. He's going to be here, and I thought you'd want to meet him."

"I'd love to!" Blythe said. "But I never received an invitation. Jamie didn't, either. I'm sure he would have mentioned it to me."

Lydia made a sound of annoyance. "The mail service is simply atrocious these days. It's a good thing I happened to see you. I do hope you'll be able to join us."

"I wouldn't miss it," Blythe assured her.

She phoned Jamie as soon as she got back to her desk, but he was out of his office and didn't return her call. He was probably in court, she surmised.

When he didn't call by the end of the day, Blythe was puzzled and a little uneasy. That wasn't like Jamie. Finally she took a chance and phoned his apartment, although it was unlikely that he'd be there.

When he answered, she exclaimed, "I've been waiting to hear from you! Didn't you get my message?"

"I was... ah... tied up." His voice suddenly filled with concern. "Is anything wrong, Blythe?"

"No, just the opposite. I met Lydia today—the saleswoman at the gallery. Did you get an invitation to the Grabowski showing they're having tonight?"

"I might have. I seem to remember seeing it."

"And you didn't tell me?" she asked indignantly.

"I guess it slipped my mind."

"You are an infuriating man! It's lucky I ran into Lydia today. You do want to go, don't you?"

"I'm afraid I can't make it tonight."

"But, Jamie, Grabowski is going to be there. This is our chance to meet him and ask about our painting. He can tell us what it's really supposed to represent."

"You can find that out on your own. You don't need me."

"I don't want to go alone. Are you sure you can't get out of whatever you're doing?" she coaxed.

"I'm afraid that's not possible. Don't you have a friend you can ask to go with you?"

A woman's voice called out to him in the background, and suddenly everything was clear to Blythe. Jamie hadn't returned her call because he didn't want to. He was afraid he'd given her the wrong idea on their last date, so he'd decided to stop seeing her.

"I have plenty of friends," she answered coolly. "Don't give it another thought. I'm sorry I bothered you."

"Blythe, dear, you know I'm always—" But she'd hung up.

Chapter Three

Blythe was furious after she talked to Jamie—both at him and herself. How could she have thought their friendship meant anything to him? He was a shallow, insincere man, and she was well rid of him. Telling herself that was one thing, but believing it was another. Under her anger was a deep sense of loss.

To shake off her depression, she decided to ask Doug to go to the gallery party with her. She wouldn't let Jamie spoil her evening. He certainly wasn't thinking about *her*. Doug was a better choice, anyway. At least he knew more about art than simply how to pay for it.

Meeting the artist took Blythe's mind off Jamie for a time. Gustave Grabowski was a big, jovial man with a beard and a twinkle in his eyes. Blythe couldn't wait to tell him she owned one of his works.

After identifying which one, she asked eagerly, "Those *are* meant to be scales in the center, aren't they? The balanced shapes and graceful curves seem so obvious to me."

He smiled. "That's why I enjoy doing abstracts. Each person sees something different."

"You mean I'm wrong?" she asked, crestfallen.

"There is no wrong or right in art. You bought the painting because it said something to you personally."

"It really did—maybe because I'm a Libra and I recognized my sign. Do you believe in astrology?"

"I believe something guides our lives, call it fate, destiny or our astral signs."

"*I* think we're responsible for our own destinies." Doug had joined them in time to hear Grabowski's statement. "Believing divine guidance will point you in the right direction is the lazy person's way out."

"How about things you can't explain?" Blythe argued. "Like meeting someone whose path had no logical reason to cross yours?"

He shrugged. "Coincidence."

After a glance at Blythe's disappointed expression, Gustave said, "Surely that's another word for preordination. I agree with the young lady. Some relationships were directed by the stars."

"Do the stars also say the relationship will work out?" Doug asked skeptically.

Gustave smiled at Blythe. "Why else would they bring people together?"

The artist's words echoed in her mind as she got ready for bed later that night. Her relationship with Jamie had come to a screeching halt, which would seem to contradict Grabowski's theory. Maybe Doug was right, and she'd met Jamie by pure accident. In any case, their friendship was over. With a deep sigh, she turned out the light.

Jamie phoned Blythe at her office the next morning, taking her by surprise. A wave of pure happiness swept over her at the sound of his voice. Then she remembered her grievance of the night before.

"I want to apologize for forgetting to tell you about the gallery showing," he said tentatively. "Did you get someone to go with you?"

"Yes, it was no problem," she answered in a cool voice. "I took Doug Ransome. He was delighted."

"Do I know him?"

"I introduced you. He's the head of the art department here."

"The big fellow who looks like a football player?"

Blythe forced herself to giggle, something she detested in anyone. "He *is* pretty impressive, isn't he? I've been dying to get him to notice me."

"It appears I did you a favor," Jamie said casually.

"Isn't it funny the way things work out?" she agreed. "I hope *your* date was as sensational."

"It was all right." He hesitated for an instant. "Would you like to have lunch today?"

Blythe was powerfully tempted, but she knew Jamie was only trying to make amends. The lukewarm invitation was proof of that. Under the circumstances, a complete break was only sensible.

"Thanks, but I'm having lunch with Doug," she said.

"He seems to be making up for lost time," Jamie remarked evenly.

Blythe managed another giggle. "I certainly hope so."

"Well . . . I'll be talking to you."

"Right. Goodbye, Jamie."

Blythe kept her hand on the receiver after she hung up, knowing it was her last contact with him. Jamie's farewell had been as final as hers.

She was weighed down all day by a sense of loss, even though she tried to tell herself that was foolish. So Jamie was gone, so what? They'd only known each other for a couple of months. She had plenty of other friends to fill the gap. People she could count on, not skittish males who bolted at the first hint of honest affection.

Blythe worked late that night because she had nothing better to do. Jamie had been taking up most of her free time. She was going to be more selective about his replacement, Blythe vowed grimly.

It was after eight when she drove up in front of her apartment building—and received a shock. Jamie was waiting for her. There was no mistaking his white Corvette. He was behind the wheel with his head resting on the seat back and his eyes closed. When he heard her car drive up, he got out and came over to her.

"What are you doing here?" She looked at him searchingly.

"Waiting for you. May I come in?"

"I suppose so." She led the way inside and flicked on the lights. "Why didn't you call first? You would have found out I wasn't at home."

"I did call. I've been phoning since six o'clock."

She gave him a puzzled look. "Then why did you come over?"

"I thought perhaps you weren't answering the telephone. I knew you were angry at me."

"Well, maybe a little. It was thoughtless of you not to mention the invitation." Her eyes shifted away from his.

"That wasn't the reason you were angry," he said quietly. "You guessed that I'd decided to stop seeing you."

"You could have told me to my face!" Blythe stopped pretending. "It wasn't fair to let me sit here waiting to hear from you. Friends don't treat each other that way."

"You're absolutely correct. My behavior was inexcusable."

"You're darn right it was," she muttered.

"It's no excuse, but the truth is, I was afraid to see you."

"That doesn't make sense," she said scornfully.

"None of this does." Jamie wandered around the room rubbing the back of his neck. "I don't know how I let it happen, but I think I've fallen in love with you."

Blythe's legs gave way, and she sank down on the couch, staring at him. "Is this your idea of a joke?"

"Believe me, I don't find anything funny about the situation," he assured her fervently.

"When did you come to this questionable conclusion?" she asked, not really trusting him. Yet why would he lie about such a thing?

"I suppose I sensed it all along, but I wouldn't admit it to myself. You're a beautiful woman. Any man would be attracted to you. I told myself that's all it was."

"How do you know it isn't?"

"For one thing, I've never been jealous before. I couldn't take it today when you told me how you felt about Doug."

"Maybe I exaggerated a little," she said cautiously.

"No, I got the message loud and clear. I can't blame you. He's a handsome guy."

"So are you," she murmured.

Blythe was a little dazed by the turn of events. Jamie's admission forced her to realize that he wasn't the only one who'd been deluding himself. She'd also fallen in love. It had seemed hopeless before; that was probably why she'd resisted the idea.

"I know you're fond of me, but that isn't enough anymore." He resumed his pacing.

"What do you want from me, Jamie?" she asked softly.

"That's the hell of it. I don't know." He ran rigid fingers through his thick hair. "Yes, I do. I want to carry you into the bedroom and undress you. I want to explore every inch of your exquisite body and bring you more pleasure than you've ever known."

Blythe shivered involuntarily. The prospect was so mind-boggling that every nerve in her body quivered.

Jamie noticed her reaction. "You don't have to worry. I won't touch you."

She rose to her feet and walked over to him. "I'm very sorry to hear that."

"Don't play games with me, Blythe," he warned harshly. "I have little enough self-control where you're concerned."

She smiled enchantingly. "I'm disappointed in you, Jamie. I thought you were a sophisticated man of the world."

"What does that have to do with anything?"

"Presumably you know something about women. Why are you so dense about me?"

"I don't understand," he said uncertainly.

She put her arms around his neck. "I fell in love, too. Probably sooner than you did."

"You really mean it?" He stared at her with incredulous joy.

Gathering her into his arms, he held her so tightly that she could hardly breathe. Then his mouth captured hers for a kiss that was torrid in its intensity. Blythe clung to him as her own passion rose to meet his. This was what she'd wanted for so long, knowingly or not.

She uttered a tiny sound of protest when he dragged his mouth away and clamped his hands on her shoulders, putting a small distance between them.

Jamie was breathing rapidly. "I swore I'd never let this happen again."

"*Why?*"

"Because it's all wrong," he answered heavily.

"You can't mean that! Why are you so determined to make us both miserable?"

"That's what I'm trying to avoid."

"You're doing a lousy job of it," Blythe declared. "How do you think I felt when you dumped me without any warning? I'm so dumb I didn't even realize what you were doing. I kept waiting to hear from you."

"I'm truly sorry about that. It was cowardly of me, but I've explained the reason for my actions."

"Not to *my* satisfaction. If you love me and I love you, I can't see the problem."

"That doesn't solve matters, it only complicates things." He jammed his hands into his pockets and turned away.

"Because you think I'll expect you to propose?" she asked evenly.

"It's a logical conclusion."

"Not necessarily," she answered dryly. "I know your views on the subject."

"You don't really believe I'm serious, though. You think I'll change my mind, and we'll live happily ever after like they do at the end of a romance novel."

"Why worry about the future when we can be happy here and now?"

"For how long, Blythe?" he asked steadily.

"I can't give you a guarantee. How long did it last with other women?" she asked unemotionally. Blythe wouldn't let herself think about the day when Jamie's ardor would cool.

"I've never been in love before. That's what makes this so difficult."

"I can't believe you've never been seriously involved with anyone," she protested.

"That isn't what I said." Jamie paused to choose his words carefully. "I've had a few close relationships. They were lovely ladies, but there was no commitment implicit on either side. We parted amicably, with no emotional damage."

"Why would it be any different with us? Surely you know me better than to think I'd hang on like a leech."

"That isn't what bothers me. I'm afraid I'd never be able to let you go."

"Then we *would* live happily ever after. Who says you have to be married to do that?"

"You're living in a dreamworld," he answered harshly. "Sooner or later, love isn't enough."

She gazed tenderly at his tortured face. Jamie was clearly suffering. And for no good reason. He would always be enough for her—with or without a wedding ring. Blythe knew with complete certainty that she and Jamie were meant to be together.

"It's enough for now," she said gently. "Why not live in the present?"

"Because it isn't fair to you. I can't let you waste your time with me, when you could be meeting someone who's able to give you what you deserve."

"Don't you think it's up to me to make that choice?"

"You're obviously being swayed by emotion."

"Too bad you won't permit *yourself* to be," she answered tartly. "Listen to me, Jamie. I refuse to let you talk yourself out of my life. I haven't had your experience, but I've dated a lot of men, and I've never found one I cared about for very long. It's different with you. Maybe I've never been in love before, either."

"Maybe you aren't now," he said morosely.

She couldn't help smiling. "Wouldn't that solve your problem? If you're right, I'll come to my senses in time and we'll shake hands and promise to keep in touch."

He pulled her to him roughly. "I can't bear to think of that happening."

"It looks as though you're between a rock and a hard place," she said calmly. "You don't know *what* you want."

He stared at her unhappily. "I must seem like a real jerk to you."

"No, just a man who's excessively wary. If I promise to love, cherish and refuse to marry you, will you stop running away from me?" she teased.

He didn't return her smile. "It isn't wariness. It's concern for you, as well as myself. I have hard evidence to prove that marriage spells the end of love. After a while two people who couldn't bear to be separated find they have no desire to be together."

"You're speaking of your parents obviously. It's sad that they drifted apart, but that doesn't have to happen. I told you about my own parents. They're living proof that you're wrong."

"I could argue the point, but it wouldn't convince either of us."

"You're right. It appears we're at an impasse." She gazed at him steadily. "You have to make the decision, since you're the skeptic. I've said my piece. I won't try to influence you any further."

A tiny smile relieved some of the strain on Jamie's face as his eyes wandered over her flawless features. "How can I look at you and not be swayed?"

She refused to use the advantage. "Then go home and think about it. You can call me tomorrow. But if you're really convinced that our relationship won't work, then we have to make the break final. Don't phone me at work, don't come over here. It's too painful, and it only prolongs the misery."

"That's true." Jamie's face was drawn as he stared at her, as though memorizing her vivid green eyes, the porcelain texture of her skin, the softly curved mouth that was quivering now, despite all of her efforts. "Goodbye, Blythe," he said quietly.

She watched him walk out the door, willing herself not to cry. Dignity was all she had left.

After he was gone, Blythe sank down on the couch, staring at the door through a blur of tears. Could Jamie have left if he really loved her? Evidently not the way she loved him. He had become the focal point of her life. What would she do without him?

After a long time Blythe went into the bedroom and got undressed. She was emotionally drained, but when she crawled into bed, the blessed oblivion of sleep refused to come. Memories of Jamie in a thousand guises tormented her. The way he looked with the wind ruffling his hair, the sound of his laughter, the glow in his eyes when he gazed at her with desire.

She turned and twisted to get rid of the tormenting images. Would she ever manage to forget him? Finally sheer exhaustion took over, and she fell asleep.

A shrill ringing sound jolted Blythe awake. In the pitch darkness she fumbled for the telephone. When a dial tone greeted her, she realized belatedly that it was the doorbell ringing. The sense of urgency made her apprehensive.

She ran to the door without bothering to put on a robe. "Who is it?" she called.

"I have to talk to you. Let me in, Blythe."

"Jamie?" She opened the door and stared at him in bewilderment. "What time is it?"

"I don't know—four o'clock maybe." He came inside and closed the door.

"What are you doing here?"

"I've been driving around all night, and I finally realized what a fool I've been. Tell me it's not too late, darling."

"For what?" She brushed the tousled hair out of her eyes.

"I can't imagine life without you! Say you'll take me back." He smothered her in an almost painful embrace.

Blythe was sure she was dreaming. She touched his face with her fingertips. It was cool from the night air, but he was definitely flesh and blood. When he kissed her with almost savage intensity, she was sure of it.

After an inflaming moment he tangled his fingers in her hair and tugged her head back. "I wouldn't blame you for throwing me out, but I'll keep coming back. I couldn't stay away from you if I tried."

Realization was finally sinking in, making Blythe deliriously happy. She laughed softly. "You did try."

"Never again," he vowed. "I've been miserable all week."

"Not completely. You managed to console yourself the night of the gallery showing."

"I was trying to forget you, but it didn't work."

"Was she very pretty?" Blythe asked in a small voice.

"I don't remember." Jamie swung her into his arms and carried her over to the couch.. The moonlight glittered in his eyes as he cuddled her on his lap. "All I saw when I looked at her was gorgeous red hair and a little tilted nose."

"I'll bet," Blythe said skeptically. "After I phoned, you probably told her I was your sister."

"The way I feel about you is anything but brotherly," he said in a husky voice.

When Jamie's lips met hers, Blythe ceased to worry about competition. His desire was unmistakable. While his mouth took deep possession, he caressed her body with great enjoyment. Since she was wearing only a short chiffon nightie, his caresses were especially arousing. Tiny flames licked at her midsection as one hand cupped her breast.

She moaned softly when his thumb gently circled the rosy tip. The thin covering of chiffon merely served to make the sensation more erotic. As liquid fire raced through her veins, she pressed against him and raked her fingers through his thick hair.

"My sweet, passionate little Blythe," he said hoarsely. "How was I lucky enough to find you?"

"Just don't leave me again," she whispered.

"You can be sure of that." Jamie's kiss was gentler this time, filled as much with love as passion.

She clasped her arms around his neck, tingling with anticipation. Jamie would be a marvelous lover. Her body was still glowing, although he was no longer stroking her sensuously.

"It's getting late," she murmured.

"I know." He sighed. "I hate to leave."

Blythe glanced up at him in surprise. "You don't have to go."

"Yes, I do." He got up and stood her on her feet. "We both know what will happen if I stay much longer."

"I thought that's what you—" She stumbled to a halt.

"What I want? More than you'll ever know." He smoothed her cheek tenderly. "But I don't want you to think that's the only reason I came back."

"I wouldn't think that. I *want* you to stay, Jamie."

"Dear heart, don't make it more difficult. I want you to be very sure. You're in a highly emotional state right now. We both are. When we make love, it's going to be for all the right reasons."

"I can think of a couple right now," she muttered.

Jamie laughed. "I could match those and raise you a few."

She wound her arms around his neck. "I'll see your bet."

"Stop trying to seduce me." He kissed the tip of her nose as he disengaged her arms. "I've never felt this noble."

"Don't expect any brownie points from *me*."

Blythe couldn't help being disappointed, but she was gratified by Jamie's concern. He didn't realize the depth of her commitment, though. She wanted to belong to him completely. He would understand that in time, and they would have a glorious life together.

From that night on Jamie was as attentive as any woman could have wished. He phoned at least once a day, but usually more often. He and Blythe saw each other four or five days a week, and sometimes he took her to lunch.

He was always ardent, even discreetly so in public. When they walked down the street, he'd hold her hand or put his arm around her shoulders. The culmination of their evenings were heated, but he always stopped short of making love to her.

Blythe was frustrated and she knew Jamie was, too, but she couldn't quite bring herself to discuss it with him. She was sure it was only a matter of time until his rigid self-control slipped. Until then, she decided not to try to rush things.

Outside of that, her life was perfect. Jamie always thought of fun things for them to do, especially on the weekends. One Saturday, he planned lunch and a round of golf at his country club, then in the evening, a revue at a theater on the neighboring peninsula. It was a full day on a rather tight schedule.

"Aren't we cutting it a little close?" Blythe asked. "I live near the club, so I'll have plenty of time to get dressed for the evening, but you'll have to go all the way to Nob Hill and back."

Jamie shrugged. "San Francisco is a small town."

"With big-city traffic. We won't have time for even a snack before the theater, with all the traveling involved."

"Maybe we can pretend we're at the movies and eat popcorn."

"I have a better idea. Why don't you bring your clothes over here?" she suggested. "While you're changing, I'll fix us something to eat. That way you won't have to rush."

"Sounds good to me, but don't go to a lot of trouble. We'll have a midnight supper somewhere after the theater."

Blythe was no match for Jamie on the golf course. He was a natural athlete with a picture-perfect swing. She enjoyed watching his supple body coil and uncoil in a fluid movement that utilized every muscle in his powerful shoulders.

Since they were only playing a twosome, Blythe indulged in a little creative arithmetic. When Jamie was marking their scorecard at the end of one hole, she said blandly, "I had a four."

"You had a five," he said, writing it down.

"How can you count that last putt?" she asked indignantly. "It was a gimme."

"You still have to count it."

"Golf is a dumb game," she grumbled. "In horseshoes I'd get points for being that close."

"What are you complaining about?" He grinned. "I gave you an extra point."

They bickered amicably as they strolled along the velvety green fairways dotted with majestic trees. Birds and butterflies circled overhead, and wildflowers dotted the woods. It had been such a lovely afternoon that Blythe hated to see it end, although the evening promised to be equally entertaining.

When they reached her apartment, she said, "I'll take the first shower so I can get started in the kitchen while you're getting dressed."

"Okay, but don't use up all the hot water," he joked.

"Cold showers are good for the character."

"I've been taking a lot of those lately," he answered ruefully.

"It's your own fault." Blythe disappeared into the bathroom, content to have made her point.

When she emerged a short time later, Jamie gazed at her with unconcealed desire. Her long hair was tied on top of her head with a pink ribbon, and her clear skin was becomingly flushed from the warm water. The short terry robe was by no means provocative, but it stopped at midthigh, revealing her long slim legs.

"It's all yours," she said. When he stared at her mutely, she added with a smile, "And I didn't use all the hot water."

Jamie strode into the bathroom without answering.

As she was about to get dressed, Blythe realized belatedly that she'd forgotten to put out a clean towel for him. She got one from the linen closet in the hall, but as she was about to call to him that it would be outside the door, he turned on the water. Since he was already in the shower, she decided to go inside and put the towel within reach.

She opened the door, then stood rooted to the spot. Jamie wasn't in the shower. He was in top physical condition, but nothing could have prepared her for the perfection of his physique. It was classic in proportion, the flowing lines broken only by a strip of white skin around his loins where his tan ended and then began again.

She drew in her breath as he reacted visibly to her scrutiny. "I . . . I'm sorry. I thought you were in the shower."

"Don't be sorry." He walked slowly toward her. "*I'm* not."

He untied her belt and pushed the robe off her shoulders. Blythe scarcely dared to breathe. As their eyes held, he took her in his arms. Their nude bodies met in a scorching embrace that acquainted her with his potent masculinity. She clung to him, melting in the heat they were both generating.

"I can't resist you anymore," he groaned.

"I never wanted you to." She moved against him in mute invitation.

Uttering a hoarse cry, he lifted her in his arms and carried her into the bedroom. When he knelt over her on the bed, straddling her legs, Blythe's heart started to race.

"You don't know how I've wanted to see you like this," he muttered. "To touch you and kiss you and make you mine completely."

"I thought you never would," she said with a sigh.

"I must have been out of my mind. You're everything I've ever wanted."

He feathered her breasts with caresses so tantalizing that she arched her body instinctively. Jamie's hands cupped her buttocks, supporting her while he strung a line of arousing kisses from her breasts down to her taut stomach. After pausing to dip his tongue into the small depression of her navel, his mouth continued its devastating path.

Blythe moved restlessly when he approached the juncture of her thighs. She twisted her legs together, but Jamie parted them gently and kissed the soft skin of her inner thigh.

"You're so beautiful, sweetheart," he murmured. "Your skin is like warm satin."

She uttered a strangled sound as he touched her intimately. "I didn't think it could be this wonderful," she gasped.

"Darling Blythe. Do you know how that makes me feel?" He stared down at her with glittering eyes. "To know I can bring you more joy than anyone else ever has."

"There's never been anyone else," she whispered.

Jamie paused and lifted his head. "You mean since we met."

"And before that. No man ever tempted me, and now I know why." She held out her arms. "I was waiting for you."

He continued to stare at her. "You're a virgin?" The passion had drained out of his face, leaving his expression unreadable.

"I thought you'd be pleased," she said uncertainly.

"It's a rather unexpected development." He levered himself off the bed.

A cold chill fingered Blythe's spine. "Does it make a difference?"

"Of course it does!" He wandered around the room, running his fingers through his hair. "I didn't realize you were completely innocent."

"You make it sound like a crime!" She sat up against the headboard and pulled the spread over herself.

"I'm sorry," he said distractedly. "It's just that you caught me by surprise."

Blythe was hurt and confused by his attitude. "I know virgins aren't rampant nowadays, but does it matter? We love each other. This isn't some casual affair."

He came over to sit on the edge of the bed. "I can't take advantage of you, Blythe. You have romantic expectations I can't fulfill."

"Because you'd feel an obligation?" she asked bitterly. "What do I have to do, give you written assurance that I'm not out to trap you?"

"I'm thinking of you, whether you believe it or not," he said gently. "I don't ever want to hurt you."

"What do you think you're doing now?" she demanded. "It's pretty humiliating to be rejected."

"It's the hardest thing I've ever done," he answered quietly.

Even in the midst of her anger and bruised pride, Blythe was achingly aware of him. Jamie was completely unselfconscious about his nudity, as he had a right to be. His virile body was magnificent. She glanced away, determined not to plead with him.

"So, where do we go from here? Are you going to disappear again?"

He sighed heavily. "That would probably be sensible, but I know I couldn't stay away. I do think you should see other people, though."

"Are you sending me out to get experience?" she asked tartly.

"Don't even joke about a thing like that!"

"That's what it sounds like. Did you have any specific number of men in mind?" she lashed out wildly, trying to wound him as he'd wounded her.

Jamie picked up his clothes and started to get dressed. "There's no point in continuing the discussion while you're this upset. I'd better leave."

Blythe couldn't force any words past the lump in her throat. She huddled on the bed, watching as he picked up his jacket and walked out the door.

Chapter Four

Blythe awoke on Sunday morning with a pounding headache after a troubled night. She'd barely closed her eyes, and even the fitful snatches of sleep hadn't brought forgetfulness. There was no escape from the humiliation and rejection she'd suffered.

When the telephone rang, making her wince, Blythe buried her head under the pillow and ignored it. She didn't feel up to talking to anyone, especially Jamie. Not until she figured out what to do about him. Could they possibly continue to see each other on a casual basis as he'd suggested? But the alternative was not seeing him at all. Either choice promised pain.

Blythe dragged herself out of bed and took some aspirin before stepping into the shower.

After she'd dressed and had coffee, the day stretched ahead with nothing to do. She and Jamie had planned to compete in a regatta organized by the yacht club. Would he go without her? Undoubtedly. Jamie had no intention of letting her disrupt his orderly life. Blythe picked up her purse and her car keys and walked out the door.

She drove around aimlessly for a while before deciding to visit Claire and her family. It had been too long since she'd spent time with them. Not since Jamie had begun monopolizing her weekends. Pushing him out of her mind, Blythe pulled into the Stonestown Mall parking lot.

Her warm welcome at Claire's lifted Blythe's drooping spirits. At least *some* people cared about her. Jenny, her niece, ran to greet her eagerly, and Claire scolded Blythe fondly.

"It's about time you paid us a visit," she said. "I was about to send you a map, in case you forgot the way to our house."

Blythe smiled. "You sound like Dad. He always said I could get lost in a phone booth."

The little girl tugged at her hand. "Do you want to see what I made in nursery school? It's a picture of Darby." A black Labrador retriever ambled over when he heard his name.

Blythe scratched the dog's ears as she examined the childish drawing Jenny had pulled out of her pocket. "It looks just like him," she declared solemnly.

Jenny stared at her work critically. "He's blacker than that, but I couldn't make him any darker with a crayon, and the teacher doesn't let us use ink."

"Maybe you'll have better luck with these." Blythe handed her the wrapped package she'd brought.

"A present for me?" The child's eyes sparkled as she tore off the gift wrapping.

"That better not be what I suspect," Claire warned.

At the same moment Jenny exclaimed, "Oh boy, a paint set!"

"They're only finger paints," Blythe told her sister hastily. "They're washable."

"Great! Are you going to come over and wash them off the walls?" Claire asked ironically.

Blythe grinned. "That's part of being a mother."

"I can hardly wait till you have children of your own, so I can get even."

Blythe's smile faltered. "Where's Bob?" she asked, changing the subject.

"He went out to get charcoal. We're going to barbecue tonight. Will you stay for dinner?"

"I was just waiting for an invitation."

"You always have a standing one." Claire looked at her questioningly. "I didn't expect to see you on a weekend. Where's Mr. Wonderful?"

"He's racing his sailboat today."

"Don't you usually crew for him?"

"Not in a race." Blythe couldn't talk about Jamie yet, not even to her sister. "It's so glorious out, let's go sit in the backyard."

"Good idea." Claire paused to call to her daughter, who had taken the paint set to her room. "Don't make a mess in there."

"I won't," Jenny's little voice answered.

"She will." Claire sighed.

"They why do you bother?" Blythe asked.

"For the same reason I tell her to wipe her feet before she comes inside, or to eat her brussels sprouts instead of trying to feed them to Darby. Because I'm an eternal optimist." Claire sank down onto a chaise. "Gee, I'm glad you came over. I've really missed you."

"I'll be over more often from now on," Blythe promised.

Claire looked at her with raised eyebrows. "That means you won't be spending all your time with Jamie. Is the romance cooling down?"

"More or less," Blythe answered evasively.

"What happened?"

"Nothing special. You know how it is."

"No, I don't. Did you get tired of him?"

"I . . . yes."

Claire was silent for a moment, obviously debating with herself. Curiosity finally won out over discretion. "I have a feeling there's more to it than that. You don't have to tell me if you don't want to, but perhaps it would help to talk about it."

"There's nothing to talk about," Blythe insisted.

"Okay, if you say so. What have you been doing since you and Jamie broke up?"

"It just happened . . . recently."

Claire gazed covertly at Blythe's shadowed eyes and drooping mouth. "How recently?"

"Last night," Blythe answered in a muted voice.

"That's too soon to decide it's all over. Every couple has arguments. It isn't the end of the world."

"This was more than a quarrel. I thought he loved me, but he doesn't." Blythe abandoned the pretense that she'd tired of Jamie.

"Did he tell you that, or are you just being dramatic?"

"He didn't have to put it into words. His actions spoke loud enough."

"I'm not quite sure what you're trying to tell me," Claire said helplessly.

"I'd rather not go into all the demeaning details. The bottom line is that Jamie is so afraid I'm trying to trap him into marriage that he suggested I go out with other men."

"That doesn't sound very promising. I think you should take him up on it."

"I suppose you're right." Blythe sighed.

"If he's too dumb to appreciate you, I say forget about him."

"How do I do that?" Blythe asked somberly. "Jamie is everything I ever wanted in a man."

"Are you sure it isn't because he's playing hard to get? Men usually sit up and beg for you. It's natural to be intrigued by one who doesn't."

"I wish that's all it was. Then I'd have some hope of getting over him. Maybe by the year 2000," Blythe added sardonically.

"I didn't realize you were this serious about him," Claire said slowly. "When I told you he was a good prospect, you said you didn't want to get married . . ."

"That was when we first met." Blythe stood up to pace the patio restlessly. "I can't say he wasn't honest with me. I knew about his hang-up from the very beginning, so how did I let this happen?"

"Don't blame yourself. Love is seldom a matter of choice."

"A lot of consolation *that* is!"

"In my opinion, Jamie is bad news," Claire stated. "But if you're that hooked on the guy, it's time to switch to Plan B."

"Which is?"

"You'll just have to change his mind about marrying you."

"I'd have a better chance of settling the conflict in the Middle East," Blythe answered derisively.

"Not necessarily. You've been so afraid of scaring Jamie off that you haven't really tried to convince him."

"Short of dragging him in front of a minister in a drugged state. What do you suggest?"

"All he sees every day are bad marriages. Expose him to a good one. Bring him over here and let him see an ideal family. Bob and I are affectionate toward each other, we have a nice house, a friendly dog and an adorable child. We're perfect role models except for one small statistic. The average American family has one-point-five children, but who wants half a child, anyway?"

"I'd take any part of Jenny," Blythe said fondly.

"There are days when I'd almost be willing to take you up on it, but Bob and I are strangely attached to her. You'll have to get your own child."

Blythe's smile faded. "That doesn't seem likely at the moment."

"I wasn't suggesting anything immediate. Start by bringing Jamie over. Pick a date, and I'll cook a dinner that will make marriage seem like heaven without the harp music."

"I saw that plot on an old 'I Love Lucy' show. Ricky came home grouchy, little Ricky spilled his milk, and if they'd had a dog, it would have bitten someone."

"How can I help you if you insist on being negative?" Claire complained.

Bob came around the side of the house carrying a sack of charcoal. He was tall and nice looking, with intelligent eyes and a warm smile.

"Hi, stranger," he said when he saw Blythe. "This is a nice surprise."

"It's good to see you, Bob." Blythe was very fond of her brother-in-law.

"You, too. Claire and I were talking about you just last night. We were wondering when we'd get to meet this guy who's taking up all your time."

"Maybe one of these days," Blythe answered vaguely.

"It must be serious. He's lasted longer than any of the others."

"Blythe promised to bring him over for dinner," Claire said.

"I didn't exactly promise," Blythe protested.

"Are you worried that we'll tell him you don't know to cook?" Bob teased.

"How can you say that? You love my divinity fudge."
Blythe was happy to lead him off the subject of Jamie. "If
I'd known I was coming over today, I'd have whipped you
up a batch."

"It's just as well," Claire remarked. "Bob is watching his
weight."

"No, *you're* watching it. Claire's been reading those
women's magazines again," he told Blythe. "How to keep
your husband healthy on five hundred calories a day."

"It seems to be working." Blythe smiled. "You're looking mighty lean and mean."

"That's hunger you see. Last night I was ready to fight
Darby for a bone, but I figured Claire would just deduct it
from my calorie intake."

While they were bantering back and forth, the front door
opened and a voice called from inside the house, "Hello.
Where is everybody?"

"It's Mom and Dad," Claire exclaimed happily. "This is
turning into a party. We're out here," she called, rising to
greet them.

Gordon Reynolds was a distinguished-looking man with
graying temples and a calm manner that inspired confi-
dence in his patients. He was the old-fashioned kind of
doctor who took a personal interest in the people he treated.

His wife, Marsha, was a small, vivacious woman with a
still-trim figure. Blythe had inherited her glorious auburn
hair and green eyes from her mother.

They all expressed pleased surprise at the impromptu get-
together, and then Jenny came running outside to add to the
commotion. For a time everyone seemed to be talking at
once.

When things calmed down a little, Bob said, "While you
all catch up on the news, I'm going to get my barbecue
equipment together. You'll stay for dinner of course," he
told the newcomers.

"Don't go to all that bother. We'll take everyone out to dinner," his mother-in-law said.

"This will be more fun," Claire assured her. "We'll hide Dad's beeper so he can eat in peace."

"That won't be necessary," her mother said. "I've finally convinced him to let his associate take over on the weekends. Now I'm trying to talk your father into going on a cruise for our anniversary. It's a big one—our thirtieth."

"That can't be!" Claire exclaimed.

"It better be, since you're twenty-nine," her mother answered mischievously.

"I find *that* hard to realize, too." Gordon smiled fondly at Claire. "I can remember so vividly the day you were born. I've seen a lot of babies in my day, but you were the prettiest."

"Until Blythe came along." Claire laughed.

"No, she was a scrawny little thing, with a face as red as her hair," Marsha Reynolds said.

"It's a good thing I had your hair color." Blythe grinned. "You couldn't disown me."

"We didn't want to." Gordon took his wife's hand. "Scrawny or not, you were a blessing from heaven."

Blythe had a lump in her throat as she gazed at her affectionate family. This was the way it was supposed to be. Would she ever achieve their kind of happiness?

"Were you always sure about each other right from the start?" she asked her parents abruptly. "I mean, did you ever have any doubts about getting married?"

"*I* didn't." Gordon looked at his wife. "How about you?"

"I wouldn't have chased you so hard if I had," she answered complacently.

"Did Dad play hard to get?" Blythe asked in surprise.

"He's a man, isn't he? Of course he did," her mother replied as her husband chuckled and shook his head, denying the accusation.

"It was all worth it, though, wasn't it?" Claire slanted a glance at Blythe.

"I guess you could say that, since we've stuck together for thirty years." Gordon and his wife exchanged a winsome glance. "It wasn't all moonlight and romance in the beginning, however. You both have to work at it if you want a marriage to succeed."

"I guess that's the key," Blythe remarked heavily. "You both have to share the same goals."

Gordon looked at her shrewdly. "Are you trying to make a personal decision?"

"No." Blythe sighed. "I think I've already made it." She forced a smile. "Who'd like to play bridge?"

Her parents looked thoughtful, but they pretended to be distracted.

"One of you girls will have to take your father for a partner, or we won't make it to our anniversary," Marsha declared. "I'll never understand how a man can recall the case history of every one of his patients, and not be able to remember how many trumps are out."

Gordon chuckled. "I play for relaxation."

"Your own, not your partner's," she answered dryly.

The afternoon passed swiftly as they played bridge, teasing Gordon when he had a memory lapse and laughing at old family jokes.

Dinner was an equally relaxed affair. They sat around the patio table, enjoying the rare treat of all being together.

When it got dark, Claire told a protesting Jenny that it was time for bed. The little girl delayed the inevitable as long as possible, making the rounds of the adults to bestow goodnight kisses.

When Blythe's turn came, she hugged the little girl tightly, feeling tears clog her throat. Why couldn't Jamie see what he was missing? The pleasant afternoon with her family had soothed Blythe, but now tension was returning. She got up to leave shortly afterward.

"Come back soon," Bob said, kissing her cheek.

"I will. Thanks for everything."

Her departure brought a flurry of last-minute reminders and expressions of affection. Finally Claire walked her out to her car.

"My invitation still stands," Claire said. "Bring Jamie over anytime."

"I don't think so," Blythe answered quietly.

"You've decided to make the break final?"

"That was your first suggestion," Blythe reminded her.

Claire looked unhappy. "I'm no expert. What if I gave you the worst advice of your life?"

"I won't hold you responsible." Blythe started the motor. "You just helped me get my head on straight."

"I hope so," Claire muttered as she watched her sister drive away.

The red light on Blythe's answering machine was glowing when she let herself into the apartment. With great reluctance she turned on the tape. As she suspected, two of the messages were from Jamie. The very sound of his voice sent a thrill through her.

"Blythe, it's Jamie." As though she wouldn't have recognized his voice, even underwater! "I hope you're feeling better this morning," he continued. "I'm sorry I missed you. Call me when you get back."

The tape continued with messages that barely registered. They were from various friends whom she was usually happy to hear from. Then Jamie's voice came on again, this time sounding more urgent.

"We have to talk, Blythe. If you're there, pick up the phone. If you really *are* out, call me as soon as you return."

She continued to stare at the phone, long after the tape had ended. Part of her longed to talk to him, even though it would only deepen her misery. Nothing was going to change the facts. He didn't love her enough to give in, even a little. This day at her sister's house had shown Blythe what she was missing—a man who wanted her more than anything else in the world. But Jamie wasn't that man.

Their relationship was over, except for informing him of the fact. Jamie was right. She couldn't keep avoiding his calls and refusing to talk to him. Squaring her shoulders, she picked up the phone. There was no sense in postponing things.

Jamie's voice held relief. "I was beginning to worry about you. You've been gone all day. Are you all right?"

"I'm perfectly fine."

Her controlled tone registered, dampening his enthusiasm. "Where have you been?" he asked hesitantly.

"I spent the day with my family. I haven't seen them in a long time."

"Oh. Well, I'm glad you had a nice day."

"It was lovely. I enjoy being with them." She wondered why she didn't just say what she'd called to tell him and get it over with.

Jamie was the one who cut through the meaningless small talk. "I'm sorry about last night, Blythe," he said quietly.

"Don't be. You saved us both from making a big mistake."

"I firmly believe that, but I can tell you still don't think so. Believe me, darling, I wasn't rejecting you."

"It doesn't matter any longer," she answered remotely.

"It matters a great deal! I never wanted to hurt you. Quite the opposite!"

"I'm sure you've convinced yourself of that."

"It's the truth. I love you, Blythe."

"You have a strange way of showing it," she said bitterly.

"Because I didn't make love to you? I explained my reasons. If I'd known how vulnerable you were, I never would have let things go that far. Unfortunately I created a physical need in you that didn't permit you to think clearly."

"I'm not having that trouble now," she answered in a clipped tone. No matter what excuse Jamie gave, she still felt rejected.

"But you don't agree with me." He sighed. "You still think I should have taken you to bed?"

"It's no longer important," she replied stiffly. Then her indignation boiled over. "But since you asked—yes, I think that's exactly what you should have done! If you loved me, that is."

"Okay. I'll come over right now, and we'll make love."

"Thanks, but no thanks," she answered coldly.

"Why? I'm offering to prove my love, since you say you're thinking clearly now."

"I don't want you anymore," Blythe said desperately. If she saw him again, if he touched her, all her hard-won resolve would evaporate.

"I'd be devastated if that were true." His voice deepened to a velvety purr. "Why don't we find out?"

Blythe's heart began to pound. They both knew what the results would be. Only last night Jamie had reduced her to a quivering supplicant with his arousing kisses and sensuous caresses over the most intimate parts of her body. But no more!

She drew a shuddery breath. "It's too late, Jamie. I called to tell you I don't intend to see you anymore."

"You can't mean that, Blythe. We have too much going for us to let it end this way."

"A clean break is better than a lot of little deaths," she answered somberly. "I can't keep going through this—fighting and making up. It doesn't solve anything."

"We don't always argue," he said softly.

"Dogs don't always bite, either. But it hurts when they do."

"I couldn't agree more. I'm miserable when we're at odds."

"Well, there you are," she said helplessly. "If all we do is make each other unhappy, what's the point?"

"Can you honestly say we haven't had some good times together?"

"No," she admitted, trying to block them out.

But Jamie wouldn't let her. "Remember the night we went dancing at the Mark? You had on a silver dress and you looked like the angel on top of a Christmas tree. I couldn't take my eyes off you."

How well she remembered. The dress was low cut and had tiny straps, so she couldn't wear a bra. The sensitive tips of her breasts had brushed tantalizingly across his solid chest while Jamie added to the erotic feeling by stroking her bare back with his fingertips.

"We closed up the place and then went to my apartment," he continued inexorably. "I cooked breakfast for you, and we ate outside on the terrace under the stars."

"Moonlight makes everything seem romantic in retrospect," she said doggedly.

"We had our share of romantic moments in broad daylight. How about the Sunday we drove down the coast and found that little secluded beach? We had on our bathing suits under our clothes, remember?"

How could she ever forget? They'd taken turns putting suntan lotion on each other. She'd applied it to his smooth skin with both palms, massaging the taut muscles in his shoulders and back while he groaned with pleasure. But when she'd followed the line of little bones down his spine to his low-slung trunks, he'd arched his body and accused her of tickling him.

Jamie had taken the bottle of lotion and stroked her back in the same way. It hadn't tickled; it was more of an itching sensation, deep inside. When he'd turned her over and smoothed the cool liquid over the upper slope of her breasts above her bikini top, the sensation intensified. Blythe always wondered what might have happened if a surf caster hadn't wandered by and decided to fish only a short distance away.

"Weren't those times worth a few rough spots?" Jamie's voice interrupted her reverie.

She hesitated. "I honestly don't know."

"Then don't make any rash decisions," he urged.

"I'm not." She sighed. "I haven't thought about anything else since last night. It seems like the only solution."

"Not if it makes you unhappy. But I'll abide by your decision. If you think you'll be happier without me, I'll leave you alone."

It was what she'd decided, but the thought panicked Blythe. "You'll be better off, too," she said tentatively. "You can't enjoy our upheavals any more than I do."

"No, but I'm not willing to lose you because of them." He chuckled unexpectedly, although it was a muted sound of amusement. "I don't look forward to our set-tos, but life with you certainly isn't dull."

"That's small compensation," Blythe declared. "I thought love was supposed to make you feel good."

"That's what I want to do, sweetheart. Don't cut me out of your life."

"You told me to go out with other men," she said uncertainly.

"I was only thinking of you. It nearly killed me to suggest it."

"You didn't really mean it?"

He paused to choose his words carefully. "It's probably a good idea. I have more toys than most men. I'd hate to think you were dazzled by them. When we make love, I want you to come to me with the full knowledge of what you're doing."

Did he honestly think she was impressed by his gorgeous apartment and fancy car? Poor Jamie, what shallow women he must have known. She'd love him if he didn't have a cent!

"You still don't know me very well," Blythe said tenderly. "Why don't you come over so we can get better acquainted?"

"I think it would be more prudent to wait until tomorrow night," he said after a moment's hesitation. "You're still pretty emotional, and I want to give you plenty of time to think it over."

"Your concern is touching, but I'd like to have a little more concrete example of your affection," she said tartly.

"Don't tempt me, angel."

"That's exactly what I'm trying to do. Did I succeed?"

Before he could answer, a man spoke to him, so close that Blythe could hear every word. "Who the devil have you been talking to for so long, Jamie? The girls are beginning to think you want us to clear out."

"Leave me alone, Kevin," Jamie said impatiently. "Can't you see I'm busy?"

Blythe became aware of something that hadn't registered before. Soft music was playing in the background. She probably wouldn't have thought anything of it if she'd noticed, since Jamie usually had the stereo on when he was at home. But now there were voices and laughter mixed with the music as people joined him from another room.

He was having a party! While she'd been searching her soul and feeling as if the bottom had dropped out of her world, *he* was enjoying himself with his friends.

Blythe became even more furious when a woman said in a cooing voice, "Come dance with me, Jamie. Peter has two left feet."

A lot of other voices joined in, too many for Blythe to catch more than a word or two. All she could tell was that it was a group of both sexes. Then Jamie put his hand over the mouthpiece. Presumably to quiet them, because when he came back on the phone, the voices were receding.

"Sorry for the interruption, darling," he said. "Where were we?"

"You were telling me why you can't come over tonight," she said sweetly. "Something about wanting me to be absolutely sure, wasn't that it?"

"That's correct," Jamie said warily. A certain quality in her voice alerted him to trouble ahead.

"Because you care about me."

"More than you realize."

"How much longer are you going to keep up this charade?" she asked angrily, abandoning her sugary tone. "We both know the real reason. You already have a date."

"Blythe, my love, you're more woman than I can handle right now. How could you think I'd want to be with anyone else?"

"I got a clue when Miss Sexpot asked you to dance."

"Mary Lou?" Jamie professed great surprise. "She's simply an old friend. As a matter of fact, she and—"

"Don't bother to explain," Blythe cut in. "I already gathered she's a good friend. I don't need to hear *how* good."

"Blythe, you can't believe—"

She stopped him again. "You're right. I can't believe I was ever naive enough to trust you. It was almost too easy, wasn't it? I can hardly blame you for getting bored."

"If you'll kindly let me finish a sentence, I can clear this up. The least you can do is give me a chance to defend myself."

"Do you deny there's a party going on at your apartment?" she demanded.

"It isn't a party. A group of friends just dropped over after the regatta."

This final evidence of his indifference was the last straw! "You've certainly had a long, pleasure-filled day," she said tautly. "I hope your night is as eventful."

"You're being totally irrational," he said impatiently. "I can't get through to you when you're like this."

"It's your last chance, because the game is over. I don't want to see you anymore, and I don't want to hear from you. Goodbye, Jamie—and this time I mean it!"

After Blythe had slammed down the receiver, she paced around the living room, venting her rage. For a while anger sustained her, but when she calmed down a little, the questions began.

Jamie kept urging her not to put him out of her life. Why? She accused him of playing games with her, but deep down Blythe knew that wasn't true. She could recall too many incidents of his tenderness and generosity. Jamie cared for her in his own fashion, but it wasn't the way she wanted.

If he really did love her as he said, it was a different kind of love from the one she felt for him. His was an idealized version that put her on a pedestal with a sign saying Don't Touch. The arrangement was very convenient for him. It was romantic, yet precluded involvement. That might satisfy Jamie, but it wasn't enough for Blythe. As much as it hurt, she knew she'd made the right decision.

Chapter Five

Jamie evidently agreed with Blythe's decision. He made no effort to contact her in the days that followed. At first she expected to hear from him, in spite of her warning. Every time the phone rang, she experienced a tangle of emotions—hope mixed with apprehension.

But after a few days of silence, Blythe knew she had to get on with her life and start seeing other men. That was easier said than done, since she was completely out of circulation. There was one person she could count on, however. Her old friend Larry Kramer.

He was gratifyingly pleased to hear from her. "It's good to hear your voice, Blythe. We've been out of touch too long. What have you been doing lately?"

"Nothing interesting," she answered. "What's new with you? Are you seeing anyone special?"

"Not at the moment. I was involved with someone, but she called it quits when she caught me cheating."

"You deserved it." Blythe couldn't keep the disapproval out of her voice. "Don't any of you guys believe in fidelity?"

"I wasn't cheating with another woman. She caught me with a lamb chop."

"Is that some new kind of fad I haven't heard about?"

Larry laughed. "Nothing kinky. Deborah is a devout vegetarian. I tried to be for her sake, but one day my carnal nature got the better of me. She found the evidence in my refrigerator—an entire rack of lamb."

"Wouldn't she give you another chance? Weak men need love, too."

"Not according to Deborah. She dropped me like a hot potato, so to speak."

"It was her loss," Blythe declared. "When are you going to stop dating these narrow-minded females?"

"When I find a gorgeous girl exactly like you."

"Look no further. I'm available every night this week."

"How did that happen? You usually have guys lined up, pawing the turf like stags in mating season."

"It's a long story," she said briefly. "How about tonight? Are you free?"

"Relatively inexpensive, anyway."

"That's okay. I'm so hard up I'll even pay for my own dinner."

"You don't have to do that. I saved a bundle on grocery money when all I bought were carrots and turnips. Suppose I pick you up at eight."

"Sounds great. I'll look forward to seeing you."

As Blythe changed clothes that night, her spirits lifted for the first time in days. Larry was a good friend, and she really *was* looking forward to seeing him. He made her laugh, which was something she hadn't done much lately.

They went to a little Italian restaurant that was an old favorite of theirs. Larry didn't even have to ask Blythe what she wanted to eat, although he went through the formality.

"Caesar salad, linguine with white clam sauce and garlic bread?"

She nodded. "With extra garlic."

"Is that your way of telling me we're not going to spend the night together?"

They had a drink first and joked back and forth the way they always did. But during dinner Larry became serious.

"Tell me what happened, Blythe. You didn't call me up out of the blue because you couldn't get another date."

"Actually that's the truth." She smiled wryly. "Redheads are out this season."

"That's a cue for me to drop the subject, but I was always a little thick-skinned." He leaned forward and took her hand. "If you need a shoulder to cry on, I have one that isn't being used."

She had never been able to fool him. Larry knew her too well. "Thanks pal, but I've done my crying," she said soberly. "Now I'm going forget about him."

"It takes time, but you'll do it. Listen to the voice of experience."

"I'm sorry. I didn't know you were a member of the club."

He shrugged. "Most people have an unhappy love affair at some time in their adult lives. If this is your first one, you've been uncommonly lucky."

"Not really. This is the first time I've ever been in love."

"Come on, Blythe! I can hardly believe that. You've gone with dozens of men."

"None like Jamie," she answered sadly.

"Was the breakup recent?"

"A few days ago."

"Oh well, that explains it. You're still suffering after-shock. Give yourself a couple of weeks. You'll wonder what you ever saw in the guy."

"If you say so," she answered tonelessly.

"What *did* you see in him? What was he like?"

"Nothing special." Blythe's smile was melancholy. "He was just tall, handsome, intelligent and extremely rich."

Larry whistled. "Maybe I'd better revise my estimate. It might take as much as a month to get over one like that."

"The possibility occurred to me."

He gazed covertly at her shadowed green eyes, veiled by drooping lashes. "Since you have some time on your hands, how would you like to meet this new guy in my office? His name is Sheldon, but don't hold that against him. His socks usually match, and he chews with his mouth closed."

"What more could a woman want?"

"Okay, so he's not exactly Robert Redford, but they do have a lot in common."

"Sheldon is a blond Adonis?"

Larry grinned. "No, but he puts his pants on the same way Redford does—one leg at a time."

"I hope your feelings won't be hurt if I pass on this one."

"At least I got a smile out of you. See, things aren't so bad."

"Not when I have a good friend like you," Blythe said gratefully.

"Let's blow this joint and go to a movie. *The Beast that Ate Cleveland* is playing at the Coronet. How's that for an upper?"

By the time Larry took Blythe home, she was feeling a lot better. Nothing had really changed, but she didn't feel so abandoned.

As they turned into her street, he remarked, "There are sure a lot of rich people in the world."

"What prompted that observation?" she asked.

"The Corvette we just passed."

Her nerves tightened, although there was no reason to think it was Jamie's. Why would it be? "I didn't notice," she answered neutrally.

"I saw one just like it when I came to pick you up tonight. Do you know what those babies cost? I went to look at one once. I would have bought it, too, except for something the salesman said."

"What did he tell you?"

"The price. Those are rich men's toys."

"It's late," Blythe said abruptly. "I have to go in."

After Larry left, she wandered restlessly around the apartment, unable to sleep. Why did Larry have to spot that Corvette? She'd managed to forget about Jamie for a few hours. Or at least to push him to the back of her mind. Now he was back, more vividly than ever. Would the pain ever ease?

Jamie haunted Blythe's sleeping *and* waking hours. She thought she saw him everywhere—on a crowded street, in a restaurant, even in the supermarket, where he'd undoubtedly never been. The merest glance of broad shoulders or the autocratic tilt of a tall man's head made her heart race.

When she came out of her office building at noon the next day and almost bumped into him, Blythe still wasn't sure her eyes weren't deceiving her.

"Jamie?" she asked tentatively. "What are you doing here?"

"Well, isn't this a nice surprise?" he remarked. "I guess our timing was just right. I have a client in your building."

"Oh. Who?" she asked, not because she cared, only to prolong the moment.

He glanced over at the roster of tenants. "Someone who works at Twembly and Trent. On the sixteenth floor."

"I thought they were attorneys, too."

"Yes, I . . . uh . . . I'm co-counsel with them on a case."

"One of your usual divorce cases?"

"Something like that," Jamie answered absentmindedly. He was concentrating his attention on her. "You're looking well, Blythe."

"You, too," she answered dutifully, although Jamie looked tired. Probably because he was dating everyone in his little black book, making up for lost time, she thought bitterly.

He hesitated for a moment. "Would you like to have lunch?"

"I thought you had an appointment."

"It won't take long. You can go ahead and get a table at Mulgrew's and I'll join you in ten minutes."

Mulgrew's was one of their old haunts. It was located in one of the many little alleys that gave San Francisco its quaintness. Tourists didn't know about the small restaurant unless they stumbled in by accident. The clientele was made up of natives who wanted a quiet place to talk over good food.

Blythe and Jamie had spent many a happy lunch hour in one of the booths there. How could she sit next to him, making small talk as though nothing had changed?

"I'm really swamped with work today," she said, not quite meeting his eye. "I'm just going to grab a quick sandwich and get right back to my desk."

"I understand." Jamie's expression showed that he did. "It was only a thought."

"Yes, well, it was nice running into you." She left swiftly and didn't look back.

The unexpected meeting with Jamie was so traumatic that Blythe dreaded a repeat. The possibility existed, however, if he had business in her building. She was a nervous wreck at lunchtime for the next few days, but their paths didn't cross again.

By Friday, Blythe had stopped worrying about another chance meeting. Common sense told her the odds were against it happening again. Jamie might even be scheduling his conferences elsewhere to prevent the possibility. If he cared that much.

When he telephoned her on Friday, she was too stunned to speak for a moment.

"Are you still there, Blythe?" he asked urgently.

"Yes, I . . . I'm still here."

"I thought you'd—we'd been cut off."

"No, but I am rather busy." She'd had time to pull herself together and realize it was a mistake to have any further contact with Jamie.

"I'm sorry to disturb you at the office, but you haven't been home much this week."

She didn't tell him she'd been spending most of her evenings working. "You could have left a message on my machine."

"I didn't think you'd return my call," he said frankly.

Blythe didn't deny it. "Then why are you calling me?"

"This is strictly a business call. The three months are up. It's your turn to have the painting."

"I'd forgotten all about it," she said slowly.

"That's hard to believe. You fought so hard to get it."

I should have let you have it, she thought silently. Who would have believed a thing of beauty could bring such ugliness. She almost hated the painting at that moment.

When she didn't answer immediately, Jamie continued, "I can drop it by your apartment tomorrow if you're going to be home."

"You don't have to do that," Blythe responded swiftly. "Just leave it with your doorman. I'll pick it up."

"It's quite heavy. You might need some help."

"I'm sure he'll put it in the car for me."

"How will you manage when you get home?"

"I'm accustomed to doing things for myself," she said crisply. "I don't need anyone."

"I envy you your self-sufficiency, but I have a vested interest in that picture. Half of it is mine, and I've become quite attached to it."

"Don't worry," she said coolly. "I'll take as good care of your half as I will of my own."

"I'm not worried. I simply intend to make sure. You could easily drop it and damage the frame. Remember when you dropped a bag of groceries and smashed an entire carton of eggs?"

Blythe's breath caught in her throat at the recollection. They had stopped at a corner market on their way home from jogging. When they reached her apartment, Jamie had set his bag down on the kitchen counter and come up behind her. He'd put his arms around her waist and slid his hands under the hem of her sweatshirt, drawing her body against his while he kissed the sensitive spot behind her ear.

"A bag of groceries is light by comparison," he remarked.

"The circumstances were a lot different," she said stiffly.

"If you say so," he answered indifferently. "I only remember the mess it caused."

"You have a convenient memory! It was all your fault in the first place."

"I didn't call to argue with you, Blythe. Just tell me what time to come over."

She could tell he wasn't going to be dissuaded. Since no hour of the day was better than any other, she decided to get it over with early.

"How about ten-thirty? That will leave the rest of the day free for both of us."

"Good idea. I'll see you tomorrow morning."

* * *

Blythe was up early the next day. After washing her hair, she applied makeup carefully, although she didn't usually bother with much more than a touch of lipstick on the weekend. She also spent a long time deciding what to wear instead of her usual uniform of jeans and an oversize sweatshirt. It was a matter of pride, Blythe told herself. Jamie mustn't think she was letting herself go because of him.

The bed was piled high with discarded clothing by the time she settled on white wool pants and a pale blue silk blouse that curved over her breasts alluringly. The outfit was casual yet sexy, but not overtly so.

By the time the doorbell rang at ten-thirty, she'd tried several different hairstyles and was still debating whether or not to use Jamie's favorite perfume. Butterflies were dancing a ballet in Blythe's stomach as she went to answer the door, but her composed expression didn't reveal the fact.

"You're right on time," she remarked.

"Promptness is one of my few virtues," he answered..

They stood and stared at each other for a moment. If Blythe hadn't been occupied with her own feelings, she would have seen the naked hunger smoldering in the depths of his eyes. But she was too busy noticing his awesome physique. Jamie was wearing the same cream-colored slacks and cashmere sweater he'd had on that first night at his apartment. Had he worn them today to remind her of a time when they'd been happy together? Not very likely.

"Where would you like this?" he asked, indicating the carved frame he'd propped against the wall.

"Just bring it inside and put it anywhere," she answered. "I'll decide what to do with it after you leave."

"I thought you were going to hang it in the bedroom."

"I might change my mind." Could she bear to look at it each night and morning, when every glimpse would be a reminder of Jamie?

"Why don't I take it in there and hold it up for you so you'll get some idea of how it will look?"

"That won't be necessary."

"You're going to need help in hanging it," he persisted.

"Okay, stick it up on the wall in here," she said desperately. "I don't care where it goes."

"I'm sorry I spoiled this for you, too, Blythe," he said quietly.

She stared at the painting through a blur of tears, unable to refute his statement. The vivid colors were just a bright smear until she blinked rapidly. Then the pattern reappeared like an old friend. The scales urged her to regain her balance.

Blythe drew a deep breath. "Maybe we should try it in the other room, after all."

Jamie followed her into the bedroom silently, where they both avoided looking at the bed. He held up the heavy frame against the opposite wall and glanced over his shoulder at her.

"About here, do you think?"

"It isn't centered. A little more to your right." After he'd complied, she tilted her head. "Down a bit. It's too high."

He moved the picture a fraction. "Is this better?"

She squinted her eyes. "Yes, that's perfect."

"Good. Get a pencil and make a mark on the wall in the middle of the frame."

Blythe tried to follow his instructions, but the painting was too large. "I can't reach the center."

"Duck under my arm."

She did as he said, but when she was inside the circle of his arms, Jamie let go of the frame. The painting slid down the wall to the carpet as he gathered her close and buried his face in her neck.

"Blythe, my love, it's been so long," he groaned.

She allowed herself one indulgent moment. Jamie's remembered embrace felt so wonderful. She relaxed against him, tilting her head back so his mouth could slide across her throat. When he turned her to face him, every instinct urged Blythe to clasp her arms around his neck, but a grain of common sense saved her.

Bracing her palms against his chest she said, "Let me go, Jamie."

"I tried that, and it didn't work."

His arms were like steel bands crushing her against his hard body. He held her so tightly that she was almost a part of him. And when his mouth closed over hers, she wanted to be.

"I've missed you so much," he said hoarsely. "I tried to stay away, but I couldn't."

Blythe couldn't hold out any longer. She freed her arms and wrapped them around his torso. "I thought you didn't care."

"Are you kidding?" He covered her face with frantic kisses. "I haven't had a decent night's sleep in weeks, I can't eat, I'm a basket case at the office. Nothing means anything without you."

"Then how could you stay away?" she asked reproachfully. "If it wasn't my turn to have the painting, you wouldn't be here today."

A glint of amusement lightened his haggard face. "It's a good thing you aren't an accountant. Math isn't one of your best subjects."

"What do you mean?"

"The three months aren't up for another two weeks."

Blythe did some rapid mental arithmetic. "You're right!"

"I was afraid that would occur to you, and then I don't know what I would have done. I was running out of excuses to see you."

"You didn't make any. That's what hurt. We haven't seen each other since we broke up, except for that accidental meeting outside my office."

He chuckled. "Is that what you thought it was?"

"Wasn't it?" she asked uncertainly. "You said you were there on business."

Jamie scooped her into his arms and carried her over to the bed. Sitting on the edge, he cradled her close.

"Darling Blythe, I've been following you like a lovesick schoolboy. It almost killed me to watch you go out with other men."

"It was only one man," she protested.

"That was one too many," he answered grimly. "I wanted to do serious damage to his smug face."

"Did you really see us? I didn't see you."

"I thought you might have. My car isn't exactly inconspicuous. I felt like a fool, but I couldn't stop myself. Even a glimpse of you was better than nothing."

"The white Corvette!" Blythe exclaimed. "Larry commented on it, but I was sure it was just a coincidence that he saw two of them in one night."

"Now you know why I haven't been getting much sleep," Jamie said wryly.

"Is that the only reason?" Blythe struggled off his lap in spite of his restraining arms. She had to think clearly, and that wasn't possible when Jamie was holding her.

"Don't you believe me?" he asked quietly.

"I think you missed me," she said haltingly. "We had a lot of fun together."

"That's a pretty pallid description of what we shared. There was magic between us." Pinpoints of light flared in his eyes as he gazed at her. "There still is. I know I'm not mistaken about that."

"I don't deny the sexual attraction between us," she began carefully. "I simply question how important I am to you."

"Good Lord, woman! I just confessed to acting like a teenager. Do you think I'd make a fool of myself if you didn't mean something to me?"

"Maybe it's just possessiveness," she answered stubbornly. "You don't want me, but you don't want anyone else to have me."

Jamie sighed. "This all goes back to the night I didn't make love to you, doesn't it?"

"Yes, but that's not the only thing that disturbs me. I was miserable after our argument. I spent all the next day thinking about you, wondering whether you really cared. But you weren't bothered a bit." Remembered bitterness colored her voice.

"If you only knew! I didn't call you first thing the next morning because I wanted to give you a chance to cool off," he said candidly.

"Is that also the reason you went sailing without me?" Blythe demanded. "I notice you didn't waste any time getting a replacement."

"What gave you that idea?"

"You told me so yourself! When I phoned that night, you said you and your friends were celebrating the regatta."

"No, I said they *dropped in* after the regatta. That was part of the reason they stopped by—to see why I didn't show."

"You didn't race?" she asked haltingly.

"I couldn't have sailed a toy boat in the bathtub," he answered wryly. "I'm never good for anything when we quarrel."

"You managed to entertain your friends," Blythe said doubtfully.

"I could hardly have put them out, but that doesn't mean I was having a high old time. You weren't alone that day, either," he pointed out.

"*I* was with my family. I wasn't dancing with another woman."

"I didn't think you were." He smiled.

"You know what I mean," she muttered.

"Yes, darling, but that's another of your misconceptions. Mary Lou asks *all* the men to dance. Her husband is a gorilla on the dance floor. Pete is an ex-football player who plows across the floor like he's going for a touchdown."

"She's married?"

"Very much so."

After a short silence Blythe murmured, "I feel a little foolish."

"You should, but if you come over here I'll forgive you."

Jamie held his arms out wide, and she went into them. He kissed her sweetly, then guided her head to his broad shoulder. Happiness flowed through her as she inhaled the clean male scent of his skin and felt the measured beat of his heart against her breast.

"I never thought we'd be together like this again," she said dreamily.

"Did you really think I'd let you go?"

"It certainly appeared that way."

"You'll never get rid of me," he declared. "I love you, sweetheart."

"I thought you didn't believe that love can last forever."

Jamie's embrace loosened as he looked at her upturned face with mixed emotions. "It can if it's treated properly," he answered after a pause. "I believe that love is like a beautiful, wild creature. It needs freedom to survive."

"Some wild creatures thrive even better in captivity."

"That isn't living, it's existing."

Blythe moved out of his arms. "Perhaps we'd better drop the subject. I don't want to argue with you again, Jamie. We both know how we feel, and neither of us is going to change the other's mind."

He gripped her shoulders hard. "I couldn't bear to lose you again. I'll try to change, if that's what it takes."

She shook her head sadly. "Your heart wouldn't be in it."

"Do you want to get married, Blythe?" he asked somberly.

"To you?" She couldn't help smiling. "If that's a proposal, it definitely needs work. Men being audited on their income tax have shown more enthusiasm."

"I'm asking you to marry me," he said doggedly.

"The answer is no. You'd throw a damper on the entire wedding party."

"I'm serious, Blythe," he said impatiently.

"So am I." Her smile faded. "I've dreamed of having you ask me to marry you, Jamie. But only if you truly want to, not because of emotional blackmail."

"I do love you," he said slowly.

"Then let's leave it at that."

"What do you mean?" he asked apprehensively.

"Let's just enjoy each other and let the future take care of itself."

He stared at her searchingly. "Will that be enough for you?"

"I don't see that I have any other option. I tried doing without you, and I've had more fun in a dentist's chair."

Jamie took her in his arms once more and stroked her hair tenderly. "I'm glad to hear my competition was such a dud."

"I didn't say that. Larry was the only bright spot in my life. At least he made me feel wanted."

"That doesn't surprise me. But his light is going to dim if he ever comes near you again."

"Don't be silly. Larry is a good friend. Besides, I was only following your instructions."

"I've just issued a new set. From now on I'm the only man in your life."

"My, my, aren't we masterful?" she teased.

"Do you mind?"

"It's one of the reasons I fell in love with you—along with the fact that I had to take you to get the painting."

Jamie glanced at the colorful canvas resting against the wall. "I owe the artist a debt of gratitude. I'm sorry I didn't get to meet Grabowski. What was he like?"

"Fascinating! He's also a very empathetic man."

"Did he confirm your hunch about the scales?"

"Not in so many words, but I think he was being careful not to commit himself. He wants people to use their imagination." Blythe looked at Jamie curiously. "You and I obviously saw different things. What attracted *you* to the painting?"

"I honestly don't know. I was just drawn to it. Perhaps it was the bright colors."

"Or perhaps it was a way for us to meet. Grabowski agreed with me that some things were meant to happen."

"I'll always be indebted to whatever was responsible."

Jamie kissed the tip of her nose and the corner of her mouth. Then his tongue traced the line of her closed lips without playfulness. She parted her lips eagerly, welcoming the symbolic entry of his tongue. He explored the moist recess leisurely at first, then with increasing urgency.

Blythe clung to him as pleasure escalated into a throbbing need. When he pulled her blouse out of her waistband so he could caress her bare skin, she whispered his name over and over again.

"My lovely, passionate Blythe. Maybe this was meant to be, too." He unbuttoned her blouse and kissed the shadowed valley between her breasts. "I want it to be so wonderful for you, darling."

She tilted her head back and closed her eyes as Jamie slid the silk blouse off her shoulders and unclasped her bra. The sensuous feeling of relaxation suddenly turned to raging excitement as Jamie's lips closed around one sensitive nipple while his thumb circled slowly over the other.

"You're so beautiful, my love," he said huskily. "I knew you would be."

"That feels so..." She anchored her fingers in his thick hair. "Don't stop. Don't ever stop!"

"Not until I fill you with joy."

As he urged her gently onto the bed, the telephone shrilled, startling both of them. Blythe's passion slowly receded as she reached for the phone.

Jamie caught her wrist. "Don't answer it."

She stared at him indecisively, but when the ringing didn't stop, she said, "It might be important."

Claire's voice greeted her. "I was just about to hang up. What were you doing?"

"I... Did you want something, Claire?"

"What kind of question is that?" Her sister's voice sharpened. "Are you all right, Blythe?"

Jamie draped Blythe's blouse over her bare breasts and kissed her cheek tenderly before getting up from the bed.

"Yes, I'm fine," she said, watching as he walked into the other room.

"You don't sound fine," Claire said suspiciously. "Are you still moping around over Jamie?"

"No, that's all over."

"I'm glad to hear it. I've thought about your situation a lot, and I've decided you were right to dump him. He doesn't deserve you."

"You misunderstood me. I meant the arguments are over," Blythe explained. "Jamie and I made up."

"Oh. Are you sure you know what you're doing? I still say he isn't good enough for you."

"You don't even know him!"

"I know he made you miserable. I've never seen you so down."

"That should tell you how much he means to me."

"I'd be happy for you if it worked both ways."

"It does," Blythe said confidently.

"Maybe. Just do me a favor. Don't rush into anything."

"People who play it safe wind up with nothing but regrets," Blythe answered impatiently. "I love Jamie, and he loves me."

"*You're* ready to make a commitment, but is he? I'm only advising you not to do anything you'll be sorry for. Jamie left you once, he can do it again."

"I was the one who made that decision."

"Which shows you had doubts."

Why did Claire have to rain on her parade? Nobody's future came with a guarantee. Wasn't it better to experience love once in your life, no matter what the cost?

"I can't talk to you right now, Claire," Blythe said abruptly. "I have something I have to do."

"All right, I can take a hint. Just think about what I said."

Blythe cradled the receiver slowly. The time for thinking was past.

Chapter Six

Jamie came back into the bedroom after Blythe had finished talking to Claire. "Who ever said the telephone was a great invention?" he asked ruefully.

"That was my sister on the phone." Blythe clutched at the silk blouse that covered her loosely, feeling slightly shy with Jamie. It was difficult to pick up where they'd left off.

"The daily phone call?" He smiled.

"I haven't spoken to her in a few days."

"You didn't have to cut her short." He sat on the edge of the bed. "We have all the time in the world."

"It's all right. I . . . I can talk to her later."

"Is something wrong, Blythe?" Jamie frowned. "What did Claire say to you?"

"Nothing important." She didn't look directly at him.

"I know better than that. Something's upsetting you. Tell me what it is."

"I'm not upset, really. I'm just a little annoyed with Claire. She doesn't seem to realize that I'm a grown woman."

Something flickered in Jamie's eyes as they glided over Blythe's bare shoulders, but he refrained from saying the obvious. "What does she want you to do?"

"It's more what she *doesn't* want," Blythe muttered.

"I see." He slanted a glance at her. "How much have you told your sister about us?"

"Pretty much everything, I'm afraid. I told you we were close."

"I gather she doesn't approve of me."

"She doesn't know you like I do."

"What advice did Claire give you? To stop seeing me?"

"Nothing that drastic. She just said I shouldn't rush into anything."

"Your sister and I aren't that far apart in our thinking. I told you the same thing."

Blythe's thick lashes feathered her warm cheeks. "That wasn't the message I got a short time ago."

"It isn't always easy to restrain myself around you." Jamie got up from the bed. "You're a beautiful woman, and I'm a normal, healthy male. I want very much to make love to you, but I think it would be a mistake while you're still hesitant."

"Did I act like I had any doubts?"

"Not at the time, but I believe your sister instilled some."

It was true in a way. Claire's words hadn't shaken Blythe's love for Jamie, but they'd heightened her insecurity. If they made love, she'd belong to him completely—in more than merely a physical sense. Shouldn't she preserve some small piece of her independence? Just in case the unthinkable happened, and he stopped loving her.

Jamie was watching the play of emotions over her mobile face. He leaned down and kissed her tenderly. "Why don't we go for a long drive? It will give us both time to think more clearly."

Blythe was touched by his perception. She threw her arms around his neck impulsively. "Oh, Jamie, I do love you so."

His arms circled her bare torso automatically. The loosely draped blouse had fallen away. After a brief moment he released her, but his eyes lingered on her small, firm breasts with regret.

"I'll go in the other room while you get dressed. The sooner the better," he added with wry amusement.

Instead of a romantic ride along the coast, Jamie drove to Bay Meadows racetrack in neighboring San Mateo. The place pulsed with color and excitement as people stood in line at the betting windows or milled around on the concourse in front of the track.

Blythe and Jamie had lunch in the stadium club overlooking the throng. The atmosphere was a little more restrained, but an undercurrent of anticipation still prevailed.

She smiled at him across the table. "This wasn't what I thought you had in mind when you suggested a long drive."

"I decided we'd be better off doing our heavy breathing over a racing form," he answered. "The stakes aren't as high"

"You're a very sensitive man," she said softly.

"And look where it's gotten me," he replied with gentle mockery.

After lunch Jamie suggested they go down to the paddock to look at the horses. He knew one of the owners who had an entry that day.

The horse's name was Midnight Star, and it suited him. His gleaming coat was the color of ebony, except for a blaze on his forehead. After Jamie had introduced Blythe to the owner and trainer, she turned her attention to the magnificent animal. Gliding her palm between his shoulders, she nodded approvingly.

"Nice straight withers." She continued down to a point above the tail. "Good croup, too."

All three men stared at her in surprise. "You sure know your horses, lady," the trainer remarked. "Are you in the racing game?"

"Only the daily rat race." Blythe laughed. "I love horses, though, and he looks like a winner."

"Count on it. This colt is ready. He's going to break fast and take an early lead," the trainer predicted.

"That's good enough for me." Jamie smiled. "Let's go get a bet down." As they walked back to the grandstand, he said to Blythe, "You never fail to amaze me. Where did you learn so much about horses?"

"From my grandfather. He bought a ranch up in Sonoma after he retired, and Claire and I spent part of every summer vacation there. While Grandpa taught me to ride, Grandma taught Claire to cook. I'm afraid she learned the more useful skill."

"Not necessarily. You impressed the pants off that trainer just now."

Blythe grinned. "If Midnight Star wins, he'll think I'm a genius."

"I already do. What's a croup? I always thought that was a children's ailment."

"The croup on a horse is the part of the rump that curves into the tail. Everybody knows that," she joked.

"The only thing I know about a horse is what side to mount from."

"I hope it's the left side. Who taught *you* to ride?"

"A riding instructor. My sister, Angela, and I were given lessons in all the social graces," he answered evenly.

Once again Blythe was struck by the difference in their backgrounds. Her learning experiences had been joyful events, because they were taught by loving relatives. Jamie was fobbed off onto paid tutors.

She managed an awkward laugh. "Well, at least you didn't have to curry your horse afterward."

"No." Jamie's lip curled sardonically. "Someone was paid to do that, too."

He was obviously making the same comparison. Blythe knew better than to offer sympathy, but she didn't know what else to say. Fortunately they'd reached the betting windows. By the time they'd conferred on how much to wager on Midnight Star, the moment had passed.

It didn't recur. The rest of the afternoon was equal to any of their better days. They scanned the racing form, which indicated a horse's problematical odds at winning, and then made bets based on hunches. As often as not, guesswork paid off, and they celebrated with champagne cocktails in the stadium club bar.

That day marked a change in their relationship. Both were determined to avoid arguments and make it work. Jamie's solution was to steer clear of situations that were fraught with danger—like private romantic interludes. They went out to restaurants and other public places, and he always kissed her good-night at her door.

Blythe knew that wasn't a permanent solution to their problem, but until Jamie could be made to see the light, she went along with it. He just needed a little time, she assured herself.

One Saturday they had a date to drive to Carmel, a charming little town a couple of hours from San Francisco. Before Clint Eastwood became mayor and put Carmel on the map, it was a small, quiet enclave of artists, beautiful homes and leisurely living. Most of the notoriety had died down since Eastwood's term ended, and it was once again a delightful place to visit.

Blythe was looking forward to browsing through the art galleries and interesting shops. They also planned to have dinner at a restaurant that had gotten rave reviews. She was really disappointed when Jamie phoned that morning to say the trip would have to be postponed.

"I'm sorry, honey, but I have to work," he explained.

"It's Saturday!"

"I know, but unfortunately this is the only day everybody can get together. I have to take a deposition in a divorce case."

"Don't they have anything better to do with their Saturdays?" she grumbled.

"If they did, maybe they wouldn't be getting a divorce," he answered sardonically.

"What's the big rush? Why can't they get divorced on a weekday like normal people, instead of lousing up everybody else's weekend?"

"I don't think that's their big concern," Jamie remarked dryly.

"Well, I guess it can't be helped. Unless you can get through at a reasonable hour. We might still be able to go. How long does a deposition take?"

"It depends on the circumstances. In an amicable divorce, it's a breeze."

"But something tells me this one isn't friendly." Blythe sighed.

"World War II was a slight difference of opinion, by comparison."

"That means you'll be tied up all afternoon?"

"I'm afraid so. Especially since my secretary is out with the flu. I have to call a temp to fill in. I just hope I get one who can read her own notes afterward."

"If you're not looking for perfection, maybe I can help out. It's been a long time since I've taken dictation, but I think I can still manage."

"That's sweet of you, angel, but there's no point in both of us wasting the day."

"It's already spoiled if I can't spend it with you."

"I feel the same way, but we'll make up for it tomorrow. We'll get an early start."

"That still leaves me with nothing to do today. As long as you're stuck, I might as well join you. It'll be fun working together."

"You obviously have never sat in on divorce negotiations. You'd have more fun trying to climb a ladder on crutches."

"I don't believe it's as bad as you make out. Besides, do you realize I've never been to your office?'

The more Jamie tried to discourage her, the more determined Blythe became. Finally he gave in, reluctantly.

Jamie's offices were a suitably elegant setting for him. The reception room was tastefully furnished with a couple of couches and some comfortable chairs. A large table in the center of the room held copies of current magazines and a tray set with bone china cups, demitasse spoons and a coffee urn.

The room was hushed now, since it was Saturday, but Blythe had a feeling this was the usual atmosphere. Beige wall-to-wall carpeting was so plush it deadened any footsteps. Blythe jumped when Jamie spoke to her from the doorway.

"I didn't hear you coming," she explained.

"Sorry. I didn't mean to startle you. Shall we go back to my office?"

She took a last glance around at the towering ficus tree in one corner and the gold-framed prints on the walls. "This room is furnished better than my living room. You must charge more an hour than my plumber."

Jamie smiled. "If you ever need my services, I'll make you a better deal than he does."

"How do you know what our arrangement is?" she teased.

"It had better be all business."

The outer door opened and a man entered, wearing a jogging suit. Blythe thought he'd wandered into the wrong office until Jamie introduced him as his client, Steven Bixby.

The man looked Blythe over with approval. "You can really pick 'em, Jamie. If this guy doesn't treat you right, you can come to work for me any day," he told Blythe.

"Miss Reynolds has an excellent job in an advertising agency," Jamie said coolly. "She's merely helping me out today because my secretary is ill."

Steve was giving Blythe his full attention. "I've been thinking about hiring an ad agency. Maybe we can discuss it later, over a drink."

"Don't you think you should get out of one entanglement before you start looking for another?" Jamie's voice was even frostier.

"Lighten up, Marshall. I'm a free man."

"Not yet, you're not," Jamie said grimly.

"He's as bad as my soon-to-be ex-wife," Steve complained to Blythe. "She gives lessons in how to take all the joy out of life."

"Let's go to my office," Jamie said. "There are a few things I want to go over with you before Lenore and her attorney get here."

"She'll be late, as usual," Steve remarked as they walked down the hall. "The only time that woman was ever on time was for our wedding. Lucky me!"

They entered Jamie's office, a large corner room with paneled walls and windows that looked out over the city and the Bay Bridge beyond. He pulled chairs up to the wide, polished desk and motioned Steve to the one next to his own.

The man grudgingly took a seat. "I don't see why we have to ruin a perfectly good Saturday with this nonsense. Lenore will do anything to make my life miserable."

"I tried to set up an appointment for next week, but you said that wasn't convenient," Jamie replied in an even voice.

"It's hard to get away. I have to work overtime to get that bloodsucking leech and her shyster lawyer off my back."

Jamie looked at him unemotionally. "I believe you told me you were going skiing."

"Oh. Did I mention that? Well, this could have waited till I got back," Steve blustered to make up for his discomfort. "I'm entitled to a little relaxation after all I've been through."

"As your attorney, let me give you some advice," Jamie said crisply. "Don't take a companion along. It would be foolish to antagonize Lenore at this point."

"Why do I have to be Mr. Clean? She isn't sitting at home by the fire, I guarantee you." After a look at Jamie's impassive face, Steve got up to pace the floor. "Okay, okay. I'll check into the lodge alone."

His tone indicated that he didn't intend to stay that way. In Blythe's opinion, his wife was lucky to be getting rid of him. Steve was the stereotypical, whining yuppie.

He stopped pacing long enough to look at his costly gold watch. "Where the hell is that woman? If she thinks I'm going to wait around here all day, she can just stuff it!"

Lenore Bixby arrived a short time later, trailing a cloud of expensive perfume. That wasn't the only thing about her that spelled money. The designer suit she wore was equivalent to a month's rent for some people, and her fingers and wrists sparkled with real jewelry, not the costume variety.

Blythe could see what had attracted Steve to Lenore, if not the other way around. She was a stunning brunette with a knockout figure and a face that could have been beautiful. It was strained now with intense emotions. Poor thing. Even though Steve was Jamie's client, Blythe's sympathies were with Lenore.

"Well, if it isn't my old sparring partner," Steve drawled sarcastically. "It was good of you to show up—finally."

His wife's eyes raked him from head to toe. "I see you dressed for the occasion. My compliments to your tailor."

Jamie and the other attorney exchanged a glance. Then Jamie took charge. "If everyone will take a seat, we can get started."

"We could have gotten started an hour ago," Steve commented. "*I* was on time."

Lenore arched an eyebrow. "Why not? It must have taken you all of about five minutes to get dressed."

"Will you lay off my clothes already? I'm sorry I'm not wearing an Armani suit, but I couldn't afford it after paying for that little number *you* have on."

Blythe hoped Lenore would point out the fact that Steve was wearing a designer jogging suit and expensive running shoes, but Jamie didn't give her a chance.

"Can we please begin?" he asked impatiently. "If everyone will cooperate, this won't take long. The community-property laws of California are clearly outlined, and we've reached a tentative agreement on alimony and child support."

"Any man who gets married in this state should have his head examined," Steve muttered

"Don't go to a brain surgeon," Lenore advised. "He wouldn't have anything to work on."

Jamie continued inexorably, as though there had been no interruption. "Now we have to agree on a division of personal property."

"I think we all agree that my client is entitled to retain her jewelry," Lenore's lawyer said smoothly.

"We damn well *don't* agree," Steve stated. "Do you know how much that stuff is worth?"

"Mr. Bixby is correct," Jamie said. "His wife's jewelry has a high monetary value. Her engagement ring alone is worth a sizable amount."

The two lawyers debated the matter, with the Bixbys joining in noisily. Finally an agreement was grudgingly reached, allowing Lenore to keep her jewelry if she gave Steve half its value from her other assets.

"How cheap can you get?" Lenore's face was flushed unbecomingly as she glared at her husband. "I wind up paying for half of every gift you ever gave me."

"At least I gave you something decent," he shot back. "Do you want half of a crummy necktie? I'll be glad to oblige."

"Don't pretend you gave me that jewelry out of the goodness of your heart," she spit at him furiously. "It was only to impress people with how much money you were making. I was a walking advertisement for your success."

"Oh yeah? Who was it who had to have diamond earrings? You wouldn't sleep with me until I bought them for you."

"I earned those the hard way!"

Blythe gazed at Lenore's contorted face with mounting distaste. She was no better than her husband. Nowhere in the discussion about jewelry was there any mention of sentiment, not even toward her engagement ring.

"I think we've covered the subject." Jamie was like the calm eye in the middle of a hurricane. "That brings us to the two family automobiles."

"I want the Mercedes," Lenore said quickly.

Steve jumped to his feet. "Over my dead body!"

"I don't need any inducements," she answered disdainfully.

He was too angry to rise to the bait. "You have your own car."

"The Mercedes is worth more than the Jaguar."

"You won't be happy until you get the fillings out of my teeth." He stared at her contemptuously before turning to Jamie. "Okay, give her the difference in price."

"I don't want money, I want the car," she said stubbornly.

"You're not going to get away with this!" Steve was almost apoplectic with rage. "I spent months having that car restored. You only want it because you know how much it means to me."

From the smug look on Lenore's face, Blythe knew that was true. What kind of person was she? Blythe's sympathy had shriveled and died long ago. She was appalled by both of them.

The day dragged on endlessly. Jamie ordered sandwiches sent in at one point, but Blythe had no appetite. She just wished for the ordeal to be over.

Finally it was. After fighting bitterly every step of the way, an agreement was eventually reached. The two attorneys shook hands without rancor, but they were the only ones. The Bixbys stormed out of the office, still trading insults.

After they'd gone, the dignified room still seemed to reverberate with the heated accusations that had been hurled. Neither Blythe nor Jamie said anything for a long moment.

She broke the silence. "That was the most disgusting display of greed and spite that I've ever seen."

"I tried to discourage you from coming," Jamie said quietly.

"You knew it would be like this?"

He sighed. "It wasn't their first visit."

"I can't believe people could talk to each other like that. They're monsters!"

"Not really. Steve and Lenore Bixby are merely a little more uninhibited than most of the couples who pass through here."

"The word is crude," Blythe said disdainfully.

"That, too." Jamie nodded. "I didn't want you to come here today because I was afraid you might think I was hammering my point home. But perhaps it's just as well you saw it for yourself. The death of a marriage isn't pretty."

"Are you trying to tell me all of your clients are like the Bixbys?" she demanded.

"No, they're an extreme example," he admitted. "But the others aren't necessarily more palatable. I've sat here and watched a supposedly cultivated husband and wife cut each other to ribbons with icy courtesy."

Blythe gazed at him uncertainly. "I don't suppose you can expect couples to feel kindly toward each other when they're getting a divorce. I just don't understand how they can want to inflict outright pain."

Jamie shrugged. "One perceived injustice leads to another, and the whole thing escalates."

"But they loved each other once." She gave him a troubled look. "How long were the Bixbys married?"

"Eleven years, and they lived together for three years before that. Steve told me."

"I suppose you think they'd still be together if they hadn't gotten married."

"Who's to say? I'm only called in after the fact."

"But you've made a decision in your own mind. Has it ever occurred to you that they didn't work hard enough at their marriage? You can't just give up when the going gets tough."

"They were together for fourteen years," Jamie reminded her.

"That doesn't necessarily prove anything," she answered stubbornly. "You don't know how long they've been fighting."

"I can scarcely believe they could live like this for years."

"It's possible. They're very superficial people. Maybe she only stayed with him because he was a good provider."

"Why did he stay with *her?*"

"I don't know. Perhaps because he knew a divorce would cost him. Steve is a very selfish man."

"And Lenore is just as bad, although she didn't marry him for his money. He didn't have any back then."

"How do you know?"

"Steve told me more about himself than I cared to hear. He and Lenore were college sweethearts, as unlikely as that seems. After college they both worked and saved every penny, first to furnish a little apartment and then so he could start his own business."

"It does sound like the all-American love story," Blythe remarked soberly. "Then where did they go off the track?"

"They turned into different people."

"Or *to* different people. Steve would make a pass at a nun, and he indicated Lenore wasn't much better. Infidelity can kill any marriage."

"It doesn't really matter what killed theirs. It's over and done with, and frankly I'm tired of the entire subject."

"Because you know I made some valid points and you don't want to admit it."

"Blythe dear, it's ludicrous for us to sit here arguing about the Bixbys. Why don't you go home and take a relaxing bath? That's what I'm going to do. I'll pick you up later, and we'll go somewhere for a pleasant dinner."

How could she just drop the subject when it was the crux of their entire relationship? Somehow she had to convince Jamie that he was wrong, that love didn't have to turn sour. Steve and Lenore were merely dreadful people.

Yet they hadn't always been, to be perfectly fair. That was the scary part. Once they'd been in love like she and Jamie. Suddenly Blythe was depressed and confused. She had to be alone to try to figure things out.

"I think I'll take a rain check on dinner, if you don't mind." She forced a smile. "The battling Bixbys gave me a headache."

"I'm sorry." Jamie looked at her searchingly. "Do we still have a date tomorrow?"

"Of course," she said brightly. "Call me in the morning."

Blythe didn't go home. She drove to her sister's house instead. Claire was in the kitchen fixing an early dinner for Jenny, because she and Bob were going out.

When she saw Blythe's sober expression, Claire groaned. "Don't tell me you and Jamie had another argument."

"Why would you think that?"

"You turn up here on a Saturday, looking like somebody just told you Santa's elves were on strike. What else could it be?"

"I *am* a little upset, but Jamie's only a part of it." Blythe told her about the events of the day.

"Good Lord," Claire exclaimed. "What an unappetizing pair."

"Jamie says they're a little worse than most, but the wrangling over every little detail is pretty standard. That's what scares me."

Claire looked at her in surprise. "How does it concern you?"

"After today I understand why Jamie feels the way he does about marriage. I can't say I agree with him entirely, but I'm beginning to wonder if love is only an illusion. Look at the soaring divorce rate. How can any two people tell if they're right for each other?"

"You don't get a money-back refund, if that's what you're looking for. You just have to plunge in and give it all you've got."

"I'm sure everyone does that in the beginning. It's the long haul I'm worried about. Have you and Bob ever—" Blythe broke off abruptly. "I'm sorry. It's none of my business."

"That's all right. I don't mind. Have Bob and I ever considered divorce? No. We've had some great shouting matches, but they simply cleared the air." Claire laughed.

"Why can some couples work out their differences, while others wind up in court?" Blythe asked plaintively.

"I think it has something to do with your immune system. Divorce is like a head cold. Everybody is exposed to them, but most people manage to throw them off."

"I was hoping for a less abstract explanation."

"Okay, look at Mother and Dad. I'm sure they had their ups and downs in thirty years, but they hung in there. Most of our friends have, too, so love does endure. How much more evidence do you need?"

"I suppose you're right," Blythe said uncertainly.

"I know I am. If I weren't already sure, you've proved it to me."

Blythe gave her a bewildered look. "How did I do that?"

"Your faith in Jamie is shaken regularly, but you never stop loving him."

"That's true," Blythe said slowly.

"Sometimes I think you'd be better off without him, but I realize you don't have any choice. True love is something you can't turn on and off. I only hope Jamie feels the same way about you."

"He does," Blythe answered quietly. "The problem is, Jamie has led a very sad life."

"Are you kidding? His idea of modest living is someone who drives a Bentley instead of a Rolls-Royce."

"Possessions don't count. He's never had the important thing—love."

"*You* love him."

"He's afraid to let himself believe that. Poor Jamie. He hasn't had much in the way of role models."

"I offered to show him a couple. What do you have to lose?"

"Maybe if all else fails." Blythe smiled.

"Well, it's your life." Claire sighed. "I just wish you were happier about it."

"I am since we had this talk. You always help me to think things out," Blythe said fondly. "I'm as bad as Jamie. I make problems where none exists."

"What do you plan to do about his hang-ups?"

Blythe grinned mischievously. "I have a few secret weapons up my sleeve."

"Show no mercy," Claire advised. "Are you seeing Jamie tonight? If not, and you're at loose ends, you can join Bob and me for dinner."

"Thanks, but I have to make a phone call." Blythe's mouth curved bewitchingly. "I have to tell Jamie my headache is cured."

Chapter Seven

Blythe and Jamie didn't discuss the Bixbys after that unpleasant day, but Jamie's guard was clearly up once more. He wasn't as relaxed with her, and his lovemaking—if it could be called that—was even more chaste.

Blythe pretended not to notice. She was as natural with him as ever, which first puzzled, then reassured him. In a very short time they were back on their old footing.

Blythe felt as at home in Jamie's apartment as she did in her own. She even kept some of her clothes there so she wouldn't have to go all the way home to change if they were going out right after work. The arrangement was also convenient on the weekend.

It was late on a Saturday afternoon when they returned from playing tennis a block from his house, stimulated from the strenuous exercise. Jamie made a pitcher of iced tea, and they took their glasses onto the terrace.

He stretched out on a chaise with a sigh of contentment. "You really gave me a workout today."

"Next time I'm going to beat you," she remarked.

"Don't count on it," he answered smugly. "I happen to be in fantastic physical shape."

"And I suppose I'm not?" she asked indignantly.

He smiled with mock lechery. "I don't know. Come over here and let me find out."

"You're not in such great condition if you can't see from there."

"I want to verify my findings." He patted the cushion. "Lie down next to me."

"In full view of the neighbors? Everybody on Nob Hill owns a pair of binoculars."

"I know, and it's our civic duty to give them a chance to use them."

"My civic duty ends at the voting booth." She walked over and perched on the edge of his chaise. Lowering her head, she kissed him briefly. "If you're through making lewd suggestions, I'm going to take a shower."

"Good idea. I'll join you."

"Promises, promises," Blythe remarked lightly, getting up.

"I meant, I'm going to hit the showers, too," Jamie said reprovingly as he followed her into the living room. "*Now* who's making lewd suggestions?"

"With no more success than you had." She laughed. "Do you think we need to take hormones?"

"Are you kidding? The ones I have are already raging." He took her in his arms and nibbled on her ear playfully.

Blythe raised her shoulder to fend him off. "Tickling is not passion."

"You're a hard sell. Okay, how's this?"

He kissed her, jokingly at first. But after a moment his arms tightened and the pressure of his mouth increased. Blythe's response was automatic. She twined her arms around his neck and parted her lips. When he deepened the kiss, her tongue dueled with his, advancing and retreating seductively. In a matter of seconds their mutual desire flamed like a bonfire.

"I've never wanted anyone so much in my entire life," Jamie said hoarsely. "Do you know how hard it is to keep from touching you?"

"Why do you try?" She blew softly in his ear before exploring the sensitive cavity with the tip of her tongue.

His rigid body stiffened even more. "You don't know what you're doing to me," he groaned.

"I'll bet I do." She pulled his T-shirt out of the waistband of his shorts and replaced it with her hands, kneading his buttocks with her fingers.

Jamie gasped and arced his body into hers. "You're playing with fire," he warned thickly. "I'm not made of steel."

She laughed softly. "I'm certainly aware of that."

With a supreme effort, he framed her face in his palms and stared into her eyes. "In another minute it will be too late. Are you sure this is what you want, Blythe?"

She looked back at him confidently. "Can't you tell?"

With a strangled cry of joy, Jamie clasped her in his arms and they sank down onto the carpet. As their bodies strained toward each other, he kissed her with a mixture of tenderness and passion.

"You're so exquisite," he said huskily, caressing her thigh under the brief skirt of her tennis dress. "I'm going to kiss every beautiful inch of you, and then I'm going to bury myself in your lovely body. This time there's no turning back."

Blythe drew a long, shaky breath. "I couldn't bear it if you changed your mind again."

"I don't think I *could* this time, even if I tried." His eyes were smoky with need. "You're never out of my thoughts.

I've lived this moment a dozen times in my fantasies, but they couldn't compare to the reality."

Blythe trembled with excitement as Jamie unfastened the tiny buttons on her tennis dress. His movements seemed agonizingly slow, and when her breasts were exposed, he stared at them with a molten expression for an interminable instant. Her anticipation soared when he lowered his head and trailed a line of tantalizing kisses around each firm mound.

She moaned softy and anchored her fingers in his thick hair as Jamie's lips closed around one taut nipple. Waves of sensation swept over her as he nibbled gently, then curled his tongue around the sensitized bud.

"That feels so... I can't even describe it." She sighed.

"That's what I want to know, my love. Tell me what pleases you."

"Everything you do," she whispered.

"Ah, darling, you're so wonderfully responsive," he said huskily.

Jamie's fingers toyed with the lace that trimmed the leg of her panties, creating a throbbing ache in Blythe that was almost primitive in its intensity. She moved restlessly, parting her legs in mute invitation.

As he traced erotic circles over her inner thigh, the doorbell rang. The rude intrusion into their private world was incomprehensible. They stared at each other in disbelief for a moment. Blythe was the first to react. She tried to sit up, but Jamie wouldn't let her.

"Just ignore it," he growled, his arms tightening.

"Who could it be?" she whispered.

"I don't give a damn who it is! They'll go away."

He lowered her head and kissed her, but she couldn't respond. The doorbell continued to peal in short staccato bursts.

"It sounds urgent," she murmured, staring up at him. "You'd better answer the door."

"It can't be anyone but George, the doorman. He doesn't let visitors come up unannounced."

"But doesn't he have a key—so he can deliver packages and things when you aren't here? What if he thinks you're out and he lets himself in?"

Jamie swore under his breath as he got to his feet. "Stay here. I'll get rid of him—possibly permanently!" he added savagely, stalking to the front entry.

Blythe ignored Jamie's instructions. She jumped up and fastened the gaping front of her dress, then went out onto the terrace, smoothing her rumpled hair.

The breeze cooled her heated cheeks, but nothing could lessen the turmoil inside of her. It was unbearable to stand on the threshold of paradise and have the gates slammed in her face repeatedly.

Jamie always seemed to get carried away at inconvenient moments, when they were apt to be interrupted. Did he plan it that way? No, of course not! He was as devastated as she at the intrusion. But this intolerable situation couldn't go on. There was no earthly reason for them to continue to be so frustrated.

Maybe they should go away together for a weekend. It would mark a significant step in their relationship, but Jamie had to resolve his doubts one way or another before they both became hopeless neurotics. She intended to put it to him bluntly as soon as he got rid of the doorman.

Blythe was so deep in thought that the voices in the living room didn't register. She was only aware of visitors when Jamie led them onto the terrace.

His face was enigmatic as he introduced the two people who accompanied him. "Blythe, I'd like you to meet my parents."

The announcement was so unexpected that she couldn't help staring at the older couple. Actually, *gaping* was a better word. Even after all the hints Jamie had dropped about them, Blythe wasn't prepared for the reality. They looked as if they'd stepped off the society page of the newspaper.

Jamie's father was a tall, elegant man with expensively styled hair. He was almost as lean and trim as his son, and his deep tan suggested he stayed that way through vigorous outdoor sports. Either that or exercise equipment and a tanning lamp.

Jamie's mother was also in perfect shape, but Blythe suspected her figure was due to rigorous dieting and regular massages. Her long scarlet fingernails weren't suited for golf or tennis, and her chic hairdo ruled out swimming.

"How delightful to meet you," the former Sylvia Marshall said dutifully to Blythe. Without waiting for a similar pleasantry, she turned to Jamie. "I hope you don't mind our popping in on you like this, Jamison dear. We wanted to surprise you."

"You succeeded," he answered grimly.

"I had a devil of a time convincing your doorman not to announce us," Fred Marshall complained. "He kept spouting a lot of foolishness about having to follow the rules."

Sylvia gave a silvery laugh. "You can imagine how far he got with your father." She inspected Jamie more closely. "Let me look at you, darling. You look absolutely marvelous. I'm glad to see you're taking care of yourself."

"Nonsense. He has plenty of time for that when age catches up with him. Youth is a time for excesses. Isn't that right, my boy?" Fred winked at Jamie. "I must say yours are agreeing with you."

Jamie ignored the comment. "What are you and Mother doing in San Francisco?"

"I flew in for the Van Slyke wedding," Sylvia answered. "Your father and I just happened to run into each other accidentally in the lobby of the Huntington. Isn't that amazing?"

"Not especially," Jamie answered. "You always stay there."

"But it was such a coincidence. I didn't even know he was in town."

"I knew *you* would be. You never miss a major social event," her ex-husband teased.

"I hated to leave Monte Carlo at this time of year, but I couldn't very well disappoint Lucy. You remember Lucy Tremaine," she told Jamie. "You used to take out her daughter, that pretty blond girl. What was her name?"

"You mean Roberta Grayson?"

"That's the one. She's Lucy's daughter by her first husband."

"Roberta is marrying a man named Van Slyke?" Jamie asked without interest.

"No, *Lucy* is marrying him," Sylvia said. "He's quite charming. I really think this marriage will take."

"She trips down the aisle with regularity. If it does take, a lot of caterers and florists will be out of business," Fred said mockingly.

"Not to mention attorneys," Jamie remarked with the same derision.

"You two are just alike," Sylvia said impatiently. "It's a good thing *some* men have romance in their souls."

"We haven't had any complaints, have we, son?" Fred chuckled. "We simply view marriage as a bonanza for the tradespeople."

Blythe had made herself so inconspicuous that the others had all but forgotten her presence. She'd listened to their brittle chatter incredulously at first, then with growing distaste. Jamie's parents were as bad as she'd suspected. All she wanted to do was get away from them as painlessly as possible.

Her tentative movement caught Jamie's attention. He moved to her side swiftly. "I'm sorry, Blythe. This can't be very interesting for you."

"It's all right," she murmured. "I know you have a lot of catching up to do. I'll leave you alone."

"Maybe that would be best." His expression was somber. "I'll call you tonight."

"You can't run off," Fred told Blythe. "We haven't even gotten acquainted yet."

"Don't be difficult, Freddy," Sylvia admonished him. "The girl probably has a previous engagement."

"Nonsense," he asserted. "She's merely being polite. I find that very refreshing." He beamed at Blythe.

"You find any young girl refreshing," Sylvia remarked without rancor. "No offense meant, Blair."

"Her name is *Blythe,*" Jamie said through gritted teeth.

"Terribly sorry, my dear." Sylvia looked at her speculatively. "Are you by any chance related to the Harrison Reynolds from Texas? They're in natural gas. So much less volatile than oil nowadays."

"We don't have any relatives in Texas that I know of," Blythe replied. "My father is a physician."

"A plastic surgeon?" Fred asked.

"No, a general practitioner."

"Too bad." Fred grinned. "If he specialized in nips and tucks, Sylvia might throw some business his way."

"You're a more likely candidate than I am," she remarked calmly. "Those bags under your eyes could stand removing again."

Jamie shoved his chair back and stood, his body taut. "I can't tell you how much I appreciate this visit. I tried to tell Blythe what you two were like, but you've done it much better than I ever could."

"You sound upset, darling." Sylvia looked at her son in surprise. "Surely Blythe knows we're only teasing each other."

"Of course she does. Lighten up, Jamison." Fred looked from his son to Blythe. "You aren't bothered by our little jokes, are you?"

"You must be very good friends," she said, not really answering the question.

"Exactly. We've known each other practically all our lives."

"Freddy was my date for my coming-out party," Sylvia remarked reminiscently.

"Only because Schyler Dunsmuir was in Europe at the time." Fred chuckled. "Schyler was the love of your life in those days."

"I was furious at him for not coming home for my debut." Sylvia smiled reflectively.

"By the time he did return, you were going with Norton Wiley, and I was madly in love with Dede Swanson."

Jamie stirred restlessly. "Could you save this ramble through memory lane for later? Blythe doesn't know any of these people."

"But I find it very interesting," she said quickly.

This was what she wanted to know. Jamie's parents certainly hadn't fallen in love at first sight. They were compatible even now, but that wasn't reason enough to get married. Did their love develop slowly? If so, what killed it?

"You both went with so many different people, it's a wonder you ended up together," she commented artlessly. "How did it happen?"

Sylvia and Fred stared at each other a trifle blankly, as though the event was slightly mystifying to them, too.

Finally Sylvia said, "I guess it was one of those things. We'd been friends for ages, but we didn't really become ro-

mantically involved until we were in a wedding party together. I was a bridesmaid and Freddy was the best man."

"We were regulars on the bridal circuit. Sylvia and I stood
up for more couples than those people who run wedding
chapels in Las Vegas."

"I really got tired of those stale jokes—always a bridesmaid, never a bride," she complained.

"You've made up for it since then, my dear." Fred smiled.

Sylvia returned his smile fondly. "We did have a lovely
wedding, didn't we? It was the talk of the town."

"My grandfather even put me back in his will." Fred
laughed. "It was the first time in years that I did anything
he approved of."

Jamie was becoming more and more restive as his parents reminisced. He glanced at Blythe often, trying to gauge
her reaction. Finally he gave up.

"Why don't the two of you have a drink while Blythe and
I get cleaned up," he suggested. "Then we'll go out somewhere for dinner."

Fred's eyes brightened. "I could certainly use a drink, but
I'm dining with some of the old crowd at the Blue Fox."

"And I'm going to the country," Sylvia said. "Maud
Skeffington is having a cocktail party for me at the Burlin-
game Country Club."

Jamie looked at his watch. "Shouldn't you get started,
then? The traffic is fierce on a Saturday."

"It sounds as if you're trying to get rid of me," his
mother answered a trifle huffily.

A little smile curved Fred's mouth as his gaze traveled
over Blythe's slender figure and long, bare legs. "Who can
blame him?' he murmured.

Sylvia's gaze followed his without the same admiration.
"I'm sure Jamison can spare a little time for his mother,"
she said tartly.

"Considering that I see you so seldom." Jamie seemed to be agreeing with her, although his expression was indefinable.

"That's so true. I wish we could spend more time together, but life is so frantic," she said helplessly.

"You've always kept busy, Mother. That was my earliest memory of you."

Sylvia seemed unaware of the irony in his voice. "You were such an adorable child," she said fondly. "No trouble at all—unlike your sister, I might add."

"Have you seen Angela lately?" Jamie asked.

"I spoke to her on the phone when I was in London a few weeks ago."

"You didn't see her?" Jamie persisted.

"I suggested lunch, but she said she couldn't get away from the store." Sylvia's mouth thinned unbecomingly. "I can't believe a girl who was given her advantages would wind up as a shopkeeper!"

"The boutique is an outlet for the clothes she designs," Jamie said evenly.

"Have you seen them? They're utterly ridiculous! I can't imagine who would buy them. Certainly nobody *I* know."

"There's a whole world out there that you know nothing about, Mother."

"Don't be impudent," she said sharply.

"I was only stating a fact. Not everyone patronizes couturiers, certainly not young working women. Angela designs clever, affordable clothes. She's quite successful, and I think you should be proud of her."

"How do you know so much about what she's doing?" Sylvia asked suspiciously.

"We keep in touch."

Blythe was as surprised as his mother. Jamie had never made more than a vague reference to his sister. Blythe was happy to hear they were close, but it was one more example of his failure to share fully.

"I don't know why she chooses to lead the life she does," Sylvia fretted. "Angela could have married any one of a dozen eligible young men."

"Cheer up, old girl," Fred said. "Marriages today are iffy things, anyway."

After the merest glance at Jamie, Blythe asked his father, "Will you be staying in San Francisco long?"

"I haven't decided yet," he answered. "I might fly back to Palm Beach if the weather here doesn't improve."

"It must be nice to be able to do whatever you please," Blythe remarked, making determined small talk.

"Freddy has always done that," Sylvia commented.

"We both did," he reminded her. "That's what made our marriage so civilized."

"We did have a better marriage than most," she said complacently. "The children never saw us argue."

Jamie rose from his chair. "I promised you a drink, didn't I?"

"Nothing for me, darling." Sylvia stood, also. "I really must dash. Can I drop you off, Freddy?"

"That would be nice." He turned to Blythe. "It was delightful meeting you, my dear."

Sylvia was reminded of her manners. "Yes, it was charming."

"Perhaps we can have dinner together one night before I leave," Fred said to Blythe.

While she was murmuring something vague, Sylvia called to him impatiently. "Come along, Freddy, if you're leaving. I'm going to be scandalously late."

Blythe remained on the terrace while Jamie walked his parents to the door. When he returned a short time later, his expression wasn't promising.

"Well, now you've met my parents," he said. "What did you think of them?"

"They were very...interesting."

He smiled mirthlessly. "Not your average mom and pop, you mean?"

"I didn't expect them to be. They lead different lives from anyone I've ever known."

"Stick with me, and you'll get a liberal education. I showed you what a nasty divorce is like. Today you saw a well-bred one."

"They did seem quite friendly," Blythe said cautiously.

"They always have been. Even when my father was chasing every female in the immediate vicinity."

"How can you say a thing like that?" she gasped.

"Because it's true. The servants used to take bets on what time he'd come home after a date."

Blythe tried not to show how appalled she was. "Did your mother finally find out? Is that why she divorced him?"

"I doubt if that had anything to do with it," Jamie answered indifferently. "I'm sure she knew about his affairs all along."

"You must be mistaken. No woman would put up with promiscuity."

"You have a lot to learn about motivation. Mother was Mrs. Frederich Marshall III. She was president of the Opera Guild, and a member of the Committee for the Performing Arts, among other good works. She went to Paris every year to replenish her wardrobe, and Dad dutifully accompanied her to all the important social events. She had everything she wanted out of life."

"Except a loving husband."

Jamie shrugged. "That was way down on her list of priorities. But I imagine they were fond of each other in their own way. It's true that we never heard them argue."

"If they were both so satisfied with the arrangement, why did they eventually get a divorce?"

"Who knows? Perhaps boredom caught up with them. She had her eye on the count and an even grander style of living among the deposed nobles of Europe, and he was probably relieved to get out of attending her endless social functions. The divorce was very amicable. Angela and I probably cared more than they did, although I can't imagine why. We didn't see any more or less of them."

"Why didn't you ever tell me you keep in contact with your sister?" Blythe asked slowly.

"You've never met her. I didn't think you'd be interested."

"I tell you about *my* sister. Does that bore you?"

"Certainly not. It's refreshing to hear about a normal family."

"I understand how traumatic the divorce must have been for you, but couldn't you try to get over your bitterness?" Blythe asked in a muted voice.

"I have. I don't think about it anymore. It all happened a long time ago."

"But it left a mark. That's the reason you're so adamant against marriage."

"After meeting my parents, how can you still have the same starry-eyed view?" he demanded.

"I never denied that some marriages end in divorce. I merely contend that they don't have to. Not when two people are right for each other."

"My God, Blythe, what does it take to convince you? Did you ever see two people more right for each other than my parents. They came from the same background, had the same friends, even their families gave their blessings. What more could you ask?"

"I didn't hear the word *love* mentioned."

"I suppose they had that, too, in the beginning."

"I doubt it. I think they got married for all the wrong reasons. Did you listen to them today, really hear their answers when I asked how they got together?"

"I've heard the story before," Jamie replied indifferently.

"Exactly—so you never stopped to analyze. As an outsider, I could see why it was a big mistake from the start."

"That's what's called hindsight," he said derisively.

"No, I could have told you so at the time. Don't you see? It was all a matter of timing and availability. Most of their friends were married, and the single life was beginning to pall. Neither of them was involved with anyone else at the time, and their families were all in favor of the idea, so why not? A big society wedding probably took months in the planning and provided plenty of excitement."

Jamie's face was austere. "You're describing very shallow people. Is that supposed to make me feel better?"

Blythe realized she'd gone too far. In her passion to show him why his values were skewed, she'd been too frank about his parents.

"I didn't mean to criticize," she said contritely. "You're right. It was only a snap judgment."

"There might be a grain of truth in what you say," he conceded. "It doesn't really matter. Every couple who gets married has a compelling reason at the time. It's only later that the reason doesn't seem as compelling," he added sardonically.

"I never met anyone with such a closed mind!" Blythe exclaimed in frustration.

"It takes one to know one," he replied caustically. "I wouldn't want you on one of my juries. You persist in ignoring hard evidence in favor of emotion."

"We aren't arguing a case. We're discussing what we believe in."

He jammed his hands into his pockets. "You already know what I believe."

"Now who's ignoring the evidence? More people stay married than get divorced."

"The statistics are narrowing."

"People aren't statistics!" she practically shouted.

"That's exactly what they are."

"How can you say that? Are you a statistic? Am I?"

"We could well become one," he replied grimly.

Blythe was overcome by a feeling of hopelessness. "Okay, Jamie, you win. I concede defeat."

"This isn't a contest, Blythe. I don't want to win," he said somberly. "I'd give anything if I could believe the way you do."

In spite of her avowed intention not to argue any longer, the temptation was irresistible. "Couldn't you keep an open mind? Your parents must have had a happy marriage for the most part. They couldn't have remained such good friends afterward."

"That isn't what I want for us—pallid acceptance! We're together here and now because we want to be. I couldn't bear to have you stay with me out of habit or pity or any other reason except a passionate desire to share my life. I wish there *was* a law that would keep us together forever, but there isn't."

"No, you can't legislate human emotions," she said sadly.

"I don't have much to offer you." His face was haggard. "I wouldn't blame you if you walked out of here and didn't come back."

"At least you've been honest with me." She turned away.

"Will I see you again, Blythe?" he asked, accompanying her to the door.

"I honestly don't know, Jamie. I'll have to think about it."

As they waited for the elevator, he said quietly, "This isn't the way I wanted this day to end."

Blythe was abruptly reminded of what might have been. She and Jamie should be in each other's arms right now, savoring the aftermath of love. That didn't bear thinking about. Not now when Jamie was so achingly close—yet so far away.

She averted her face and stepped wordlessly into the waiting elevator.

Chapter Eight

Blythe spent a predictably miserable Saturday night, trying to figure out what to do. She'd resisted calling Claire, because this was a decision she had to make for herself.

Common sense told her that Jamie was right. She ought to end the torment once and for all. He had practically told her they had no future together. How much plainer could he get? But then she remembered the suffering on his face—and little things started coming back to her, like the reasons he gave for ending the relationship.

Jamie said he couldn't bear to have her stay with him out of pity. Blythe stopped her furious pacing as a riveting thought occurred to her. He didn't question his own love; he questioned hers!

Jamie had never seen real commitment between a man and a woman, so naturally he doubted its existence. His parents had stayed together for reasons that any normal person would reject.

Blythe resumed her pacing up and down the living room. How could she convince him that their love was not only real, but indestructible? Look at the tests it had survived in the short months they'd known each other. The problem was, words didn't convince him. He was a lawyer, trained at countering arguments. He demanded evidence.

Blythe thought deeply for a moment, then nodded her head in satisfaction. Okay, she'd give him evidence. She would show him how normal couples behaved toward each other—not the freaks he dealt with. Claire was right all along. Jamie needed to see loving marriages at work.

Blythe's brow creased in thought. It would be a little too obvious to take him to Claire's for dinner, as her sister had suggested. Naturally her own family would put on a good act. Besides, she wanted to overwhelm him with proof. But how?

Finally the solution came to her. She'd give a party. Valentine's Day was on Friday. What could be more appropriate?

Blythe was so excited that she almost called Claire to discuss the plan, until a glance at the clock told her it was almost two in the morning. Since she was also too excited to sleep, she got a pad of paper and a pencil and began to make a list of people to invite.

Sue and David, definitely, and of course Stephanie and Craig. Everyone teased them about acting like honeymooners, even after two years of marriage. The list grew as Blythe wrote down every happily married couple she knew.

By the time she finished, it was quite late, but she was still too keyed up to sleep. Knowing she needed to unwind first, she took the newspaper and got into bed. It served its purpose; after a short time she became drowsy. Her eyelids were drooping as she read one last item, her horoscope. "Libra—Sept. 23–Oct. 22. Don't let past disappointments make you too cautious. Dare to try something new. You will be pleased with the result.''

Blythe's mouth curved in a beatific smile as she turned out the light.

Jamie called at nine the next morning, waking Blythe out of a deep sleep. She was so disoriented that while she fumbled blindly for the phone, her answering machine clicked on.

Jamie left his message in a somber voice. ''I doubt if you went out this early, so I assume you don't want to talk to me. I can't blame you. I won't bother you again.''

That jolted Blythe fully awake. She hastily grabbed the telephone. ''Jamie, wait! I'm here. Don't hang up.''

''You didn't have to answer, Blythe,'' he said heavily. ''I understand.''

''I wasn't avoiding you, Jamie. I was asleep.''

''I'm glad *somebody* got some sleep,'' he muttered.

''I got to bed very late,'' she explained.

''You went out?'' he asked tautly.

''No, I . . . uh . . . I had things on my mind.''

''I'm not surprised.'' After a pause he asked, ''Did you come to any conclusion?''

''Several of them.''

''Are you going to tell me, or let me twist slowly in the wind?'' Jamie sounded as if his nerves were stretched to the limit.

Blythe's heart went out to him, but she couldn't help being gratified by his suffering. It was proof of how deeply he cared. She was right about that.

''What did you decide about us?'' he asked urgently.

''To begin with, I think we should lighten up.''

''What does that mean?''

"We've had wonderful times together, but it's always been just the two of us. I've only met a few of your friends, and you've never met *any* of mine."

"Is that really important right now?" He was clearly impatient at the digression.

"I think so. If we went out with other people occasionally, we wouldn't spend all our time worrying about where our relationship is going."

"You want to date other men." His voice was grim.

"Not necessarily. What I had in mind was expanding our social life to include other couples."

"If that's what you want, although I don't see how it will solve anything."

"I think it's worth a try. If nothing else, we'll get to see all the people we've been neglecting," she added lightly.

"I'm afraid I've been selfish," he said in a muted voice. "I haven't wanted to share you with anyone."

Blythe ached to tell him she felt the same way, but he had to be convinced she was no longer that serious about their relationship. It was too bad if it made him unhappy, but the results would be worth the temporary pain.

"I'll do anything you say," he promised. "I'm just glad you haven't cut me out of your life completely."

"I couldn't do that." She gave a little laugh. "We own property together."

"The painting is yours. I never intended to take it back."

"I couldn't accept it," she protested. "It's worth a lot of money."

"That's the only thing I have to give you," he replied sadly.

Blythe kept her voice brisk to cover the lump in her throat. "Well, let's not worry about it now. My three months isn't nearly over. It's a good thing, too, because I've decided to have a party Friday night, and I want everyone to see it. You're invited, naturally. Can you come?"

"I suppose so." His tepid answer was caused by surprise, which he quickly mastered. "Yes, of course I'll be there."

"Good. I'm hoping Claire and Bob will be, too. You've never met my sister."

"No, but I'd like to."

"It's rather short notice for them. They're often booked up weeks in advance. But if not this time, you'll meet them some other time." Blythe's dismissive tone indicated it wasn't important one way or the other.

"I hope they're available. I've heard so much about your sister."

"She's one of a kind," Blythe said fondly. "But there will be lots of other people you'll like. At least, there will be if I get busy and start phoning them. I have a million things to do today."

Jamie hesitated for an instant. "Then I'd better let you go."

Blythe had purposely indicated she'd be tied up all day. It was partly true, but she didn't intend to see him for the remainder of the week, either. Their relationship was too volatile right now. She didn't want anything to flare up and prevent him from attending the party Friday night.

Propping a couple of pillows behind her head, she dialed Claire's number.

"What are you doing up so early on a Sunday morning?" Claire asked.

"I'm not up." Blythe stretched luxuriously. "I'm lying in bed making phone calls."

"That's right, rub it in. I've already put a load of clothes in the washer and cooked breakfast for a husband, a child and a dog."

"What do you cook for a dog?"

"The same thing you cook for the family if he's as spoiled as ours. Why are we discussing Darby's diet? Are you thinking about getting a dog?"

"I wasn't planning to, although I'd like to have one. It would be nice to have something warm and cuddly to greet me when I come home."

"Get a husband instead," Claire advised. "They can also help with the dishes and they don't shed on the couch."

"Neither does a dishwasher."

"A man has other capabilities that I was too delicate to point out. And speaking of husbands, how is Operation Jamie progressing?"

"We'll soon find out. I've decided to take your advice," Blythe told her.

"Which gem of wisdom is that?" Claire asked cautiously. "I seem to remember changing my mind a couple of times."

"The one about exposing Jamie to a happy marriage."

"I'm glad you're finally taking a positive step. Just tell me the night and what you want for dinner."

"I'm not bringing him there. I want you and Bob to come here."

"Are you planning to extract a deathbed proposal from Jamie when he thinks he's dying? You're a terrible cook."

"I might not be in the gourmet class, but I'm not that bad," Blythe protested.

"Oh no? The fire department goes on red alert when they know you're in the kitchen."

"Stop exaggerating. Besides, I won't be doing the cooking. I'm going to hire a caterer."

"For a little family dinner? What's going on, Blythe? That wasn't what I suggested. How is that going to impress Jamie with the simple joys of married life?"

"It won't be a little family dinner. I'm having a cocktail buffet with all my friends in attendance—my *married* friends."

"I'm beginning to see the light, but wouldn't my original plan be simpler? A party is so hectic. The message might not get across."

"It will," Blythe answered confidently. "In a much subtler fashion. Jamie would catch on in a minute if I tried to pass you off as the ideal family."

"Well, thanks a lot!" Claire exclaimed indignantly.

"You know what I mean. It would look staged. This way he'll meet a lot of terrific people who could be out playing the field, but who prefer being married. He'll get the point without my hammering him over the head with it."

"I hope your plan works," Claire said dubiously.

"It has to. This is my last chance."

"Did you set yourself a time limit or something?"

"No, I met Jamie's parents and discovered what I'm up against," Blythe answered soberly.

"He took you to meet his parents? That's a hopeful sign."

"It was an accidental meeting. They dropped in at Jamie's apartment while we—" Blythe checked herself hastily. "We'd just returned from playing tennis. His mother looked fantastic in a Chanel suit and real pearls, and I had on a rumpled tennis dress."

"I scarcely think she held that against you. People who play tennis get sweaty."

"That wasn't the problem. It was their total absence of affection toward Jamie. They might have been two charming, attractive people who just happened to drop in on a friend."

"Maybe they were simply inhibited because you were there," Claire commented.

"These aren't insecure people, believe me! I felt so sorry for Jamie. If his own parents don't care about him, how can he believe love exists!"

"I'm sure they love him." Claire couldn't conceive of any other circumstances.

"Perhaps in their own fashion, but that isn't good enough. He has to find out that his kind of family is the exception. I want to show him how *we* all feel about each other. I just wish I could think of some way to have Jenny here on Friday night."

"I suppose it wouldn't be the end of the world if she stayed up late one night."

"No, you wouldn't have any logical reason to bring her." Blythe declined the offer regretfully. "And Jenny would be sure to tell everyone it was her first grown-up party."

"You're right about that. There's no telling what she'd say to Jamie. She's heard us discussing him."

"That does it! Jenny is definitely off the guest list."

"She can be your ace in the hole if you need some arm-twisting."

"I'm afraid this is my last gasp," Blythe answered with a deep sigh. Then her spirits lightened. "Will you help me with the party? I need the name of a good caterer."

"Leave everything to me. Just tell me how many people you're having, and I'll take care of the rest."

"How can I ever thank you?" Blythe asked gratefully.

"Get married and make me an aunt."

"I'm trying as hard as I can."

Jamie phoned Blythe often during the following week, but she fended off all his invitations with the excuse that she was busy with the party.

"You have to eat lunch," he persisted. "At least we can see each other for an hour. Meet me at Mulgrew's."

"I really can't, Jamie. I have an appointment with the caterers."

"I thought you saw them yesterday."

"Yes, well, I . . . uh . . . I decided to change the menu."

"Receptions at Buckingham Palace are given with less preparation," he complained.

"But they do it all the time. This is the first party I've given in ages."

"And the last for a while, I hope," he grumbled. "I haven't seen you all week. I miss you, angel."

"I miss you, too, darling, but we'll get together soon. I have to go now."

"Blythe, wait! How about dinner tonight?"

"I really can't. I have a million things to do."

"If you're having the party catered, what do you have to do?"

"All kinds of things. I need to get out my good dishes and wash all the glasses that have been gathering dust on the top shelf of the cupboard." Before he could bring up any other objections, she said hurriedly, "I'm due at a meeting, Jamie. I really must run."

The enforced separation she'd imposed was as hard on her as it was on him. But Blythe was buoyed up by expectations of the party—and its aftermath.

Jamie would stay on after the others had left, and they'd discuss the guests. He was bound to have some favorites among them. Then Blythe would comment, ever so casually, on how happy those couples were. Well, no, maybe that would be too obvious. Perhaps she'd remark on what full lives they led, how they managed to have plenty of time for their careers, their children and each other. Or whatever. Something would occur to her.

Jamie would be all relaxed and mellow. He'd hate to leave her and go home to an empty apartment. He was bound to make the contrast between the warm companionship they'd shared and the solitary life he lived.

They'd kiss affectionately—she'd be careful to keep her responses in check. But the chemistry between them always erupted. Jamie wouldn't be able to control himself. His caresses would become more intimate, more urgent. And then...

Judging by her past luck, a guest would return for something he or she had forgotten, Blythe thought with dark humor. She dismissed the errant notion impatiently. This time everything was going to turn out the way it was supposed to.

Blythe left the office early on the day of the party, although Claire assured her that everything was under control. It hadn't been an overstatement.

Blythe scarcely recognized her own apartment. It was decorated with red-and-white paper streamers, and a long buffet table held a centerpiece of red and white roses. Appetizing aromas were coming from the kitchen, where unseen people were bustling around. Claire was putting the finishing touches to the living room.

"It looks fantastic in here," Blythe gasped. "You didn't tell me you were going to do all this."

"It's a holdover from the days when I was always on the committee to decorate the school gym for dances. I developed a crepe-paper fetish." Claire tilted her head to view her handiwork. "You don't think I overdid it, do you?"

"It's perfect. Everyone will be in a festive mood the minute they step through the door."

The telephone rang and was picked up in the kitchen. "That reminds me," Claire said. "Your friend Melanie called. She and Jim can't make it tonight."

"What a shame!" Blythe exclaimed. "I really wanted them here. Did she say why they can't come?"

"Their baby-sitter disappointed them at the last minute, and they can't find anyone else."

"Why don't they simply bring the baby?"

"Do you think that's a good idea?" Claire asked doubtfully. "He's only, what—nine or ten months old?"

"It's a perfect idea!" Blythe's eyes sparkled with excitement. "They're so adorable at that age."

"Sure, they don't talk yet."

"Exactly. All they do is coo and look angelic. Jamie can't help being captivated."

"I thought you said having children around would be too heavy-handed."

"Mikey isn't a child, he's a baby. And this isn't a setup. There's a perfectly valid reason for him to be here. I'm going to phone Melanie right away."

Blythe had bought a new dress for the occasion. It was pink silk, with a very short, full skirt. The wide portrait neckline just grazed her shoulders, revealing an alluring amount of creamy skin.

She'd brushed her long auburn hair to one side and secured it with a circlet of pearls, leaving the shining length to flow down her back and over one shoulder.

A pair of spike-heeled pink sandals completed the outfit. As she finished spraying herself with perfume, the doorbell rang.

Jamie was the first to show up. "I've been told it's as bad form to arrive early as late, but I couldn't wait to see you." His eyes glowed as they roamed over her. "You're as ravishing as I remembered," he said in a husky voice.

"It hasn't been *that* long." Blythe tried to laugh, but her breath caught in her throat.

Jamie was positively stunning in a dark suit, custom tailored to his tall, lithe body. The white shirt emphasized his deep tan, which made his eyes an even more brilliant blue. This man could dazzle any woman, from eight to eighty.

"It seems like forever." He caressed her cheek so lightly that she barely felt it. "I want to take you in my arms and kiss you, but you look too perfect to touch."

"Looks are deceiving," she murmured, moving closer.

"Not yours. You're absolute perfection." He lowered his head and kissed her bare shoulder, then slid his lips along her throat.

A woman came out of the kitchen. She was dressed in a black uniform with a little white apron. "Excuse me, Miss Reynolds, but can you tell me where the wine opener is? We've looked everywhere and we can't find it."

"I'll get if for you." Blythe looked ruefully at Jamie. "I'm sorry."

"Not nearly as sorry as I am." He sighed. "Will I ever get to be alone with you again?"

"Later, darling," she promised. "After everyone's left."

"I'll hold you to that." His eyes locked with hers.

Blythe's spirits were soaring as she started for the kitchen. Everything was working like a charm. This was going to be a night to remember.

When the other guests started to arrive, Blythe didn't have as much time to spend with Jamie. She introduced him to everyone, but then she had to leave to greet new arrivals. Jamie wasn't neglected, however. Her friends were intrigued by him, first because of his elegant appearance, then by his great charm. Blythe was delighted by his instant acceptance, although she'd never doubted it.

When she introduced Jamie to her sister and brother-in-law, there was mutual curiosity on all sides.

"It's good to finally meet you." Bob extended his hand. "Blythe has told us a lot about you."

"She's talked about both of you a great deal, too." Jamie looked at Claire. "Especially you. I envy you your close relationship."

"Siamese twins are only a little bit closer." Bob grinned. "Don't tell Blythe anything you don't want Claire to know."

"My husband is exaggerating," Claire said evenly. "Blythe and I do sometimes discuss the men she dates, but only in an impersonal way."

Bob looked surprised. "I thought she was only seeing Jamie." After his wife sent him the universal warning look that all husbands understand, he said hastily, "But what do I know? I can't keep up with Blythe's love life. She has men waiting in line to take her out." As Blythe stifled a groan, Bob made matters worse. "The guy who gets her is going to be one lucky man."

"You and Jamie have a lot in common," Blythe remarked swiftly. "You both like to barbecue." It was a clumsy segue, but the best she could do on the spur of the moment.

"I thought you lived in an apartment," Bob said to Jamie, as anxious as Blythe to change the subject.

Jamie concealed his amusement at the general discomfort. "I do, but I'm fortunate enough to have a terrace. Actually I mostly use the barbecue as a heater on cool nights."

"I never thought of that," Bob said. "Do you use wood or charcoal?"

Blythe and Claire drifted away. "I suppose you know I'm going to do serious damage to your husband," Blythe whispered.

"I don't blame you. I'll testify at your trial. I swear, I don't know what got into that man."

"Poor Bob, he thought he was being helpful." Blythe sighed. "I don't think any real harm was done, though."

"What if I tell Jamie that Bob played football without a helmet, and we just pretend he knows what he's talking about?" Claire suggested.

"What if we leave well enough alone?" Blythe countered.

The party was a big success. Good company and good food combined to put everyone in high spirits. The few glitches were unfortunate, but perhaps inevitable.

After circulating among all the guests, Blythe joined a group that included Jamie. Everybody was convivial, but the conversation soon took an alarming turn.

"Do you realize you're the only single man here?" David Bronson asked Jamie.

Jamie smiled easily. "Blythe could scarcely ask a married man to be her date."

"Not with all her friends as witnesses."

"That isn't funny, David," Blythe said sharply. "I've never gone out with a married man."

"It was only a joke," he answered placatingly.

"I remember being single," a man named Scott remarked reminiscently. "Stopping off after work to unwind over a drink. Watching Monday-night football without guilt."

"Coming home to an empty house and having to cook your own dinner," his wife, Lauren, commented.

"What's the big deal? I just sent out for pizza."

Blythe could cheerfully have throttled him. *She* knew Scott and Lauren were happily married, but that wasn't the impression he was giving. She stole a worried glance at Jamie, but his expression was bland.

"Blythe taught me how to order pizza the first night we met," he said.

Even Craig, the perennial honeymooner, joined in the sabotage. "Pizza is only one option. There's Chinese takeout, deli, the frozen-food section at the supermarket. You can zap an entire dinner in the microwave in five minutes."

"If you guys are so self-sufficient, why did you bother to get married?" Lauren asked acidly.

"I wouldn't touch that question with a pointed stick," her husband, Scott, replied, to general male laughter.

After a glance at Blythe's expression, Lauren said, "Okay, you fellows have had your fun. Now tell Jamie how you really feel."

"Or sleep on the couch tonight." When Scott saw that his wife was really annoyed, he put his arms around her. "I'm only kidding. The truth is, Jamie, single life is like your teenage years—they were great at the time, but you sure wouldn't want to repeat them."

"That's true." Craig gazed at his wife lovingly. "I didn't know what real happiness was till I got married."

Blythe gritted her teeth. Even to her ears, they sounded phony. It was ironic that they were telling the truth now, but Jamie was probably more convinced when they were kidding around. Blythe was grateful when the doorbell rang and she had an excuse to leave the group.

A young couple entered the apartment, offering a flurry of apologies. The woman was carrying a baby wrapped in a blue blanket printed with little white bunnies.

"I'm sorry we're late," Melanie Hoffman said. "Michael was so fussy that we almost didn't come at all. I think he must be teething."

Blythe gazed at the rosy-cheeked baby who made a happy gurgling sound. "Mikey couldn't be fussy, could you, you sweet thing?"

"Oh no? I'll call you in the middle of the night when he reaches his full-decibel power," Jim Hoffman told her wryly.

Most of the other women gathered around, making cooing sounds and admiring comments.

"He's simply adorable, Melanie."

"Look at those big blue eyes, and did you ever see such gorgeous skin?"

"Can I hold him?" Blythe asked.

Melanie transferred the bundle to Blythe's arms. "We brought his car bed. I'll have Jim put it in the bedroom."

David and Jamie were watching the commotion. "Melanie really timed her entrance right, didn't she?" David asked indulgently. "The kid's the highlight of the party."

"His presence is hard to overlook," Jamie agreed sardonically.

"It's funny the way babies bring out the maternal instinct in women," David mused. "Even the ones who aren't especially interested in having one."

"The same thought occurred to me," Jamie answered.

Blythe looked up and saw him watching her. She brought the baby over to him. "Isn't he precious?" she asked.

Jamie glanced briefly at the child in her arms. "Very nice."

"Is that the best you can do? Mikey happens to be an outstanding baby. Look how angelic he is."

As though to prove her wrong, the infant stirred fretfully. His face puckered, and he started to cry. Blythe spoke soothingly to him, but his wails only got louder.

"I wonder what's wrong with him?" she asked helplessly.

Jamie's face wore a mocking expression. "Not everything goes according to plan."

She was too distracted to hear him. While she was trying to quiet the child, Melanie took him out of her arms, laughing at Blythe's look of alarm.

"Don't worry, he probably needs changing. I'll take him into the bedroom."

Everybody was having such a good time that no one wanted to leave. The last guest straggled out reluctantly, well after one o'clock.

Claire and Bob were among the last to depart. While Bob was saying good-night to Jamie, Claire took Blythe aside.

"I must admit I had my doubts, but you really pulled it off," she said. "I never saw so many happily married couples in one place."

"Do you think Jamie was impressed?" Blythe whispered.

"How could he help but be? *I* was. If I weren't already married, I'd rush out and tie the knot."

"I only hope he has the same reaction," Blythe said wistfully.

"He should be all softened up by now. Bob and I will get out of here so you can score the final point."

"You do approve, then?"

"The man is an Adonis. Whatever you do, don't let him get away. They don't make that model anymore."

Bob came over to join them. "Can we go home now?" he asked his wife plaintively. Giving Jamie a baffled look, he remarked, "I'll never know what women find to talk about so much."

Jamie's smile didn't reach his eyes. "Men aren't supposed to understand women. They don't really want you to."

"That's good to know. Now I can stop trying." Bob kissed Blythe's cheek. "Great party, kid." He took his wife's arm. "Let's get out of here before Blythe asks us to stay and help her clean up."

"I think she can handle everything by herself," Claire answered demurely.

Chapter Nine

When Blythe and Jamie were alone, she happily surveyed the shambles of her living room. "I think it was a success, don't you?"

"They all enjoyed themselves, if that was your object."

She was too keyed up to question his phrasing. "The caterer Claire got for me was marvelous. Weren't those Swedish meatballs delicious?"

"Yes, they were excellent."

"They left the kitchen spotless, too. I won't have to do a thing in there."

Jamie glanced around at the crumpled paper napkins littering tables, along with a collection of used glasses. Adding to the general disorder were the crepe-paper streamers that were beginning to sag in places.

"You'll have enough work in here to make up for it," he commented.

"I'll clean up tomorrow. Sit down and tell me what you thought of my friends."

"They were very cooperative—except for a few lapses here and there."

She gave him a quizzical look. "What is that supposed to mean?"

"You went to a lot of trouble, Blythe. I suppose I should be flattered."

"I have no idea what you're talking about. Didn't you have a good time? I thought you were enjoying yourself."

"I was. My admiration for you is boundless. You planned each detail masterfully."

Jamie's strange behavior was beginning to make her uneasy. "I did put a lot of thought into this party," she said slowly.

"It showed, believe me."

She felt a tiny chill creep up her spine. "Why doesn't that sound like a compliment?"

"I meant it as one. You have qualities I never suspected."

"Would you like to tell me what this is all about, Jamie?" Blythe asked evenly.

"The party, of course. I was meant to be impressed, wasn't I?"

"I didn't pretend to cook the food," she answered warily.

"You know that's not what I mean." Jamie's mocking expression was replaced by one of austerity. "It was quite a coincidence that everyone here tonight was married. I assume you do know some single people. Why weren't any of them invited?"

"No special reason." Her pink cheeks would have given her away, even if her shifting gaze didn't. "I just thought you'd like these particular people. I'm sorry if you didn't. They're all good friends of mine."

He ignored her pretense of hurt feelings. "I could tell that. The women were briefed better than their husbands, however. The look on your face was priceless when they spoke wistfully of bachelor life. Fortunately their wives reminded them of how miserable they'd been," Jamie added sarcastically.

"Men always talk that way. I suppose they think it's funny. Anyone who wasn't paranoid on the subject of wedlock would realize they weren't serious."

"If you're so sure of that, why did it upset you to have me hear their little jokes?"

"Because you look for every opportunity to point out that marriage doesn't work. I showed you it does."

"You admit that was the purpose of the party," he said triumphantly.

Blythe's simmering anger came to a boil. "I'm not on the witness stand. I don't have to defend myself."

"You can't!" His anger flared to meet hers. "We may have differing opinions, but I never thought you'd resort to trickery to make your point."

"Don't you think you're overreacting? So I invited all married couples to a party, how is that underhanded?"

"What about the baby? That was an inspired touch. You knew how you'd look, holding him in your arms."

"Whether you believe it or not, that wasn't staged. Most *normal* people like to hold babies. I'm sorry if it bothered you."

"What really hurt was finding out you're like all other women," Jamie said bitterly. "You'll resort to any means to get what you want."

"Don't take it personally, pal," Blythe answered furiously. "That doesn't include you."

"You've changed your original plan? I can't wait to see the next one," he drawled.

"You aren't part of it. I wouldn't have you now if you begged me!"

"Then I won't bother. Too bad you went to all this trouble for nothing."

"It wasn't wasted. I found out once and for all that I was in love with someone who doesn't exist."

Jamie's mockery vanished and his eyes held pain, but he didn't dispute her statement. "Luckily you found out in time to look for someone who does."

The realization that he meant what he said was devastating. Blythe's own anger dissolved into misery. "I won't be in any big hurry after this experience."

"I guess that's understandable. We both got burned."

"At least I still believe in enduring love," she said quietly. "Maybe not for us, but I know there's such a thing."

"I'm glad I haven't destroyed your faith along with everything else."

"For your sake as much as mine, I wish I could have convinced you," she said sadly. "I'm sorry for you, Jamie, but I can't help you."

"I'm sorry, too, Blythe," he said heavily "Sorrier than you'll ever know. I wish I could lie to you and tell you I'll change, but I can't."

"I appreciate your honesty, anyway."

His face was tortured as he gazed at her, memorizing every feature. "You'll find someone who really deserves you."

How could any man ever take Jamie's place? Blythe's nails bit into her palms as she willed herself not to cry. This was the last time she'd ever see Jamie, and she didn't want him to remember her that way.

"Don't worry about me." She raised her chin gallantly. "I'm a survivor."

"I envy you." He sighed.

Blythe's endurance was almost at an end. "I don't think there's anything left to say."

"You're right. I should leave." Although Jamie agreed with her, he remained where he was, unwilling or unable to go. "If you ever need anything, Blythe, anything at all, you can call me—day or night."

"You know I won't."

"No, I suppose not." He moved finally, then paused at the door. "I'd like to think we're still friends."

"Certainly." She would have agreed to anything that would make him leave. Her nerves were ready to snap.

"Maybe I could call you now and then," he said tentatively. "Just to keep in touch."

"*No!* Don't do that." Blythe took a deep breath to steady herself. "We both know it's over, Jamie. Why drag it out?"

"You're right, of course." A welter of emotions coursed over his face as he stared down at her. Almost involuntarily he reached out to touch her cheek, then quickly dropped his hand. "Goodbye, Blythe. Take care of yourself, and have a good life."

When the door closed behind him, Blythe leaned her forehead against the panels, feeling utterly drained. At least she'd resisted the urge to plead with him—or to use more effective tactics.

If she'd put her arms around his neck and pulled his head down to hers, Jamie probably wouldn't have been able to resist. Neither of them had ever denied the awesome chemistry between them. They might have patched things up one more time, but that would only prolong the agony. It was over.

Finally Blythe moved away from the door and straightened her taut body. In an effort to blot out the sorrow, she began to put the living room back in order. After getting a tray from the kitchen, she gathered up all the crumpled cocktail napkins and used glasses. She put the glasses in the dishwasher, then pushed the furniture back in place and removed the paper streamers from the walls.

Trying to keep her mind a blank, she vacuumed the rugs and waxed the tables. She even got out a bottle of spray cleaner and removed smudges from the doors.

When there wasn't anything left to clean, Blythe went into the bathroom and took a hot bath. It didn't relax her as it was meant to. All the emotions she'd been suppressing fought their way to the surface, drowning her in misery.

What would she do without Jamie? He'd become the focal point of her life. She'd always believed he could be won over, that someday they'd get married and have children like all the other couples who loved each other.

But Jamie didn't really love her. She'd tried to tell herself he did, that he was simply gun-shy. It went deeper than that, however. He was incapable of making a commitment. That was why she had to sever all ties to him. Otherwise the future would hold a series of these agonies, and she couldn't live like that.

It was almost five o'clock when Blythe finally crawled into bed. She ached in body and spirit, but sleep didn't come to ease the suffering. She stared at the ceiling, dry-eyed, until the sun came up. It dispelled the darkness in the room, but not in her soul.

The telephone started ringing early. Blythe listened stoically as the answering machine took messages from her friends, telling her what a good time they'd had.

"Fantastic party, Blythe! Such a good group."

"Great party. Everybody certainly enjoyed themselves."

Blythe smiled sardonically as she remembered one guest who hadn't. What a good actor Jamie was. The next caller confirmed it.

"Really liked your friend, Jamie," Sue said. "I was expecting an announcement all evening. He's really crazy about you."

Melanie's call rubbed salt into the throbbing wound. "Jim and I had a wonderful time. I want to thank you for insisting we bring the baby."

Blythe got out of bed and took the phone off the hook. She went into the kitchen, made coffee and tried to read the newspaper. When she remembered to put the phone back on the hook about an hour later, it started to ring immediately and the machine answered. Blythe picked up the receiver this time because Claire's voice came on. She wasn't ready to talk to anybody, not even her sister, but she knew Claire would persist until she reached her.

"I waited till late to call because I thought you'd be sleeping in, but your phone's been busy all morning," Claire said.

"Yes, I got a lot of calls."

"I don't doubt it. The party was smashing."

"Thanks to you." Blythe attempted to sound cheerful. "Your decorations really set the mood."

"I always think they help." Without pausing, Claire asked, "So? Don't keep me in suspense."

This was what Blythe had been dreading. She clenched the receiver. "About what?"

"Stop acting coy. About what happened last night after Bob and I went home. What did you think I wanted to know? Whether you had any food left over?"

"As a matter of fact, I do. Would you like the rest of the pasta salad?"

"If you don't want it. Bob loves it, although it isn't on his diet."

"Pasta's not supposed to be fattening."

"The dressing on it is."

"That little bit can't hurt him."

"Will you tell me why we're discussing pasta?" Claire demanded. "You know what I'm waiting to hear."

"Not now, Claire," Blythe pleaded. "I'm tired and I have a million things to do."

"I don't like the sound of that. If everything had gone according to plan, you'd be dying to talk it over."

"I'm tired of talking. That's all I've been doing all morning," Blythe lied.

"You told everyone else before you told me!" Claire exclaimed in outrage.

"I didn't tell anybody anything. There's nothing to tell."

"You mean, Jamie didn't propose?" Claire sounded disappointed. "Didn't you even discuss it?"

"The subject came up." Blythe's knuckles were white from clenching the phone. "We agreed to wait awhile before deciding anything definite."

"Was that your idea or his?" Claire asked suspiciously.

"It was a mutual decision."

That was the first truthful thing Blythe had said. She knew it was pointless to avoid telling her sister what had happened. Claire would find out sooner or later. But Blythe simply couldn't relive the trauma this soon.

"Don't try to kid *me*," Claire said. "You let that man sweet-talk you again. I don't know why you allow him to get away with it time after time."

"Last night you told me he was the greatest thing to come along since home mail delivery," Blythe observed sardonically.

"I said he was spectacular, but I didn't advise you to let him dangle you like a puppet on a string."

Blythe's eyes were bleak. "He knows he can't do that anymore."

"Did you have an argument? What happened after we left?"

"We talked."

"That was your first mistake. The man is an attorney. Didn't you ever hear that actions speak louder than words?"

"Do we have to discuss this now?" Blythe asked tautly. "I have a terrible headache."

After a pause Claire said in a chastened voice, "I'm sorry. I didn't mean to crowd you. Get some rest, and call if you need me."

Blythe felt a rush of gratitude for her sister's unquestioned support. It was what she badly needed right now. Nothing could change the situation, but suddenly Blythe craved a sympathetic ear to pour her troubles into.

"As I'm sure you've guessed, Jamie and I are through," she said quietly.

Claire stifled a sigh. "You must admit you have a habit of overreacting, Blythe. I'm sorry you two argued again. I really thought all signs were go last night, but you should be used to these minor setbacks by now."

"This wasn't one of our ordinary arguments. I know I've said that before, but this time it's true. Believe me."

"How did it start?" Claire asked patiently, obviously *not* believing her.

"Over the party. It's ironic that I thought it would solve all my problems." Blythe gave a bitter laugh. "I guess in a way it did."

"Jamie didn't like your friends? Someone said something nasty about lawyers? What lit his fuse?"

"None of those things. I simply wasn't as clever as I thought. Jamie realized that all of the couples there were married. He accused me of using them as bait to trap him."

"Well, that's not too far off the mark. Too bad he was alert enough to catch on. But couldn't you sort of laugh it off and tell him he should be flattered that you cared enough to go to all that trouble just for him?''

"Jamie said it first, only he made it sound like a cold-blooded plot. He said I was like all other women. That really hurt.''

"So knowing you, you lost your temper.''

"Wouldn't you?'' Blythe demanded.

"Anybody would,'' Claire soothed. "I can see how things got out of hand, but it's silly to blow the incident out of proportion. You both said a lot of things you didn't mean, and now you're sorry. Jamie probably called to apologize and got the busy signal all morning.''

"You don't understand, Claire. We've already apologized to each other. It's over.''

"You're right, I *don't* understand. If you made up, why the gloom and doom?''

"We aren't angry anymore. That would mean there's some hope, but there isn't. Jamie told me to find someone else, and I realized it was the only solution.''

"He actually told you that?'' Claire asked incredulously. "*After* you stopped fighting?''

"Yes.''

"I don't know what to say.'' Claire sounded helpless for once.

"He was being straightforward with me. Jamie is as unhappy as I am over the breakup. He cares for me, but not enough to share his life or even his deepest emotions. I can't settle for half a man, and that's all I'll ever get from him.''

"I'm so sorry, Blythe.''

"I am, too. I've heard that love is hell, now I believe it.''

"I know Jamie is special, but you'll find someone else.''

Blythe's mouth twisted humorlessly. "Please don't say someone who deserves me.''

"I gather that line's been taken.''

"Along with the one about needing a man who appreci-ates me," Blythe said mockingly.

"Too bad the truth comes out sounding like a cliché. Be-cause it *is* the truth. You're a terrific person. You should have someone whose head isn't all messed up. Look around. There are hundreds of guys who fit the description. You can get any man you want."

"Not any man."

"Forget about Jamie," Claire said impatiently. "Get on with your life."

"Just like that? How simple you make it sound."

"That was thoughtless of me. Of course you're not go-ing to forget him overnight. But you *will* get over him. Trust me."

"I don't suppose I have any other choice." Blythe sighed.

"Just promise you won't take him back when he realizes what a jerk he's been and tries to talk you into taking up where you left off."

"He won't. Jamie couldn't stand going through this tur-moil again, either."

Claire wasn't as sure. "But if he does come back, prom-ise you won't weaken. Remember how you feel today."

"I'm not likely to forget. Don't worry, Jamie is a closed chapter in my life."

"Good. Now let's talk about the party. I loved the dress Sue had on. That color would look terrific on you." Claire knew that Blythe couldn't have cared less about the party, but at least it got her mind off herself for a short time.

Her instinct was correct. At first Blythe had to force her-self to respond, but after a while she did forget her trou-bles. Or at least she stopped dwelling on them.

When Claire could tell that Blythe was in a calmer frame of mind she said, "Well, I'd better go make lunch for my hungry horde. How about coming over and joining us?"

"Thanks, but I'm not dressed yet."

"No problem. I'll save something for you, even if I have to fend Bob and Darby off with a chair and a whip. You can eat whenever you get here."

"I don't think so. I'm not really hungry."

"Would you rather I came over there?" Claire dropped her bantering tone. "I don't want you to be alone."

"Don't worry, I'll be all right."

"I do worry. You're my kid sister."

Blythe was warmed by Claire's concern. She could always count on her family. Poor Jamie. He didn't have anyone to comfort him in his hour of need. Blythe closed her mind to the bleak picture. He wasn't her concern any longer.

"I'll be over shortly," she told her sister.

Claire had obviously briefed Bob on what had happened. He was so solicitous that Blythe didn't know whether to laugh or cry. In spite of their efforts, or maybe because of them, it was a difficult day for Blythe. She was emotionally drained when she got home that night—they'd insisted she stay for dinner, too—but sleep still eluded her.

After tossing and turning for hours, she bunched the pillow under her head and muttered, "What's the big deal? It isn't as though you're not used to sleeping alone."

Sunday was a little better because Blythe didn't have to keep up appearances. She told Claire she was going to spend the day with friends, then went out and took a long, solitary walk.

Getting over a painful love affair was like recovering from the flu, she told herself doggedly. It just had to run its course. Even though you might feel as if you were going to die, sooner or later you got better.

Her pep talk held hope for the future, but didn't do a lot for the present. Blythe had never been so glad to see Monday arrive. She needed to immerse herself in work. The Rice Crunchies account was going to get more than its money's worth that day.

Blythe was the first one in the office that morning. She got out the cereal-account file, sharpened all the pencils in the cup on her desk and took the cover off her typewriter. Then she sat and stared at it.

What would make people buy Rice Crunchies instead of its competitors? There were many brands on the market similar to it. The trick was to make this cereal seem irresistible. The way some people were irresistible to each other.

Blythe frowned and picked up a pencil. Rice Crunchies were good for you. So what? That never carried any weight. The bad things were the ones that were attractive. You could know something would hurt you and still yearn for it, with all your heart. She shoved her chair back abruptly and went to get a cup of coffee.

Blythe was back at her desk, staring fixedly at the folder in front of her when Doug entered the office.

"You're here early," he remarked. "What gives?"

"I woke up early, so I decided I might as well come to work."

"Did you have a nice weekend? You were throwing a party, weren't you?"

"Yes." She shuffled some papers around, hoping Doug would see she was busy.

He didn't take the hint. Perching on the edge of her desk, he asked, "Was it a good party?"

"I guess so. None of the guests got drunk or put a lamp shade on their head."

"That's a standard gag, but I wonder if anyone ever did it," Doug mused.

"I can't imagine it, but you never really know people, even if you think you do," Blythe answered somberly.

"Very profound. Can I credit you with that line?" He grinned and slid off the desk. "I'd better get started on the Blue Satin layout."

Blythe did her work mechanically. She took phone calls and sat in at a meeting, although she didn't contribute much. A crushing sense of weariness weighed her down.

At lunchtime, when everyone else went out to a restaurant or gathered in the lunchroom with their brown bags, Blythe stayed at her desk. She hadn't accomplished much that morning, in spite of her early start, and she wasn't really hungry, anyway.

It was about two o'clock when Phil Preston, one of the vice presidents, came storming into her office. "I just spoke to the printer. He promised us a rush job on those posters for the Mainwaring account if we got the transparencies to him by 9:00 a.m., but they never arrived. What the hell happened?"

Blythe stared at him in confusion. "I don't know."

"What do you mean, you don't know? You were supposed to send them over by messenger."

"I was?" Blythe faltered.

"It's *your* account! Mainwaring was promised those posters first thing tomorrow morning, but there's no way we can deliver them now."

"I'm sorry," Blythe whispered.

"Don't tell *me*, explain it to *him*. The guy's a real pain in the you-know-what to begin with. He'll scream his head off. This isn't like you, Blythe."

"I'm sorry," she repeated.

To her horror, she felt tears clog her throat. She'd held herself tightly in check for days. Was the dam finally going to burst here, of all places? She bit her lip till it hurt.

Phil's annoyance vanished when he saw her reaction. "Hey, don't take it personally. You know me, I'm a screamer, too."

"No, you're right. I goofed."

"We all do once in a while. It's no big deal. Maybe the printer can still get those posters out by tonight if we get the stuff over to him right away. How much time does he need? We're not asking him to etch hundred-dollar bills."

"I'll get on it right away." Blythe had composed herself through great effort.

He looked more closely at her. "Are you okay, Blythe?"

"Yes, I'm fine." She was already dialing for a messenger.

Phil waited until she hung up. "You look like you're coming down with something. You have dark circles under your eyes."

"I haven't been sleeping well, that's all."

"Maybe you should take a few days off."

"It isn't necessary, honestly," she insisted.

"Well, at least take the afternoon off. That's an order."

Blythe didn't really want to go home. What would she do there? But she certainly wasn't doing any good here. Maybe taking a few days off was a good idea. It might help her get her head on straight.

Not at home, though. She needed to get away, go someplace that didn't hold memories of Jamie. But where? After a few moments the solution occurred to her. She reached for the telephone and dialed her sister's number.

"You caught me as I was going out the door," Claire said.

"I'll make it quick," Blythe promised.

"That's okay, I can spare a few minutes. Did you have a good time yesterday?"

"What did I do yesterday?" Blythe asked blankly.

"You told me you were spending the day with Sue and David."

"Oh. Yes, it was very nice." Blythe didn't pause for questions. "I have a favor to ask."

"Anything. You know that."

"Can I borrow your house at Stinson Beach for a few days?"

After a moment's hesitation Claire asked, "For yourself?"

"Naturally for myself. I wouldn't ask you to lend it to anyone else."

"You want to go down there alone? At this time of year?"

Blythe finally realized what was bothering her sister. "Yes, I'll be alone. I'm not going with Jamie."

Claire didn't bother to hide her relief. "Then of course you can have the house. I was just afraid you were planning a romantic reunion by a roaring fire, and I didn't want to be a party to it."

"You won't be. I'm going there to get *away* from Jamie."

"But all by yourself? I hate to see you do that, Blythe. If you can wait about a week, I'll make arrangements for someone to take over here and I'll go with you."

"Thanks, but I need to get away now. And—no offense—I need to be alone. You've been a tower of strength and I truly appreciate it, but I have to sit down by myself and figure out what I'm going to do with the rest of my life."

"I understand, and I know you'll come through this okay," Claire said fondly. "But if you get lonesome, just give me a call."

"I'll do that. Can I come by for the key now?"

"I won't be here. One of the kids at Jenny's nursery school is having a birthday party, and I promised to help keep the little angels in line. I'll be home by five, though, at the latest."

"I was hoping to leave earlier than that. I'm not crazy about driving down that twisty road in the dark."

"I should hope not," Claire declared. "You're not familiar enough with it."

"I really want to start right now. Could you leave the key for me someplace?" Blythe suggested.

"Where is my head?" Claire exclaimed. "You don't have to come all the way over here. Mrs. Halstead, my neighbor down there, has a key."

"She doesn't know me," Blythe said doubtfully. "They weren't living there the last time I came for a visit. Do you think she'll give me the key?"

"I'll call and tell her it's all right. Got to run now. Relax and forget your troubles—and drive carefully."

Blythe followed the second part of Claire's instructions, of necessity. The winding road took all her concentration. On the left, beyond a steep drop, was the Pacific Ocean, wild now in winter. Foam-tipped waves churned restlessly in their rush to dash themselves against the shore. The view was breathtaking, when Blythe could spare a moment from watching the road.

At the bottom of the mountain was a wide sandy beach, deserted in the gathering dusk except for wheeling gulls and slender-legged sandpipers.

Claire's house was on a bluff overlooking the ocean. There were other houses on the street, but most were closed for the winter. Light shone out of only two of them.

Blythe was puzzled, because the one she'd thought was Claire's was lit up. Probably she was confused by the darkness, which was rapidly falling. Mrs. Halstead would point her in the right direction. Blythe stopped her car in front of the neighbor's house.

There was a Mr. Halstead, too. They were an older, retired couple who lived at the beach year-round. They'd been alerted and welcomed Blythe hospitably.

"Your coloring is different than Claire's, but there's certainly a family resemblance," Dora Halstead remarked after they'd gotten acquainted. "We're so fond of your sister and brother-in-law and that darling little girl."

"Come over to the fire," Carl Halstead urged. "It's nippy down here at this time of year. Can I pour you a brandy?"

Blythe declined tactfully. "I'd like to get unpacked and settled in. I'm rather tired."

"I don't doubt it. You've had a long drive." Dora handed her the key.

"I haven't been down here in quite a while, and I seem to have gotten confused," Blythe said. "I thought Claire and Bob's house was the one on the left, but there are lights on in there."

"We turned them on," Carl explained. "I also lit the furnace and laid a fire in the fireplace for you. All you have to do is light a match to it."

"And you'll find a few little things in the refrigerator, so you won't have to rush out to the market," Dora told her.

"How very kind of you!" Blythe exclaimed.

"We do it for Claire and Bob all the time," Dora answered deprecatingly. "Go along and have a nice hot bath. You look all tuckered out."

As a result of their thoughtfulness, Blythe entered a warm, welcoming house. After taking the recommended bath, she had a snack from the refrigerator and lit a fire in the big stone fireplace in the living room.

Curling up on the couch, she stared at the crackling fire, trying to count her blessings. Family, good friends, a job she enjoyed—everything but the one person she needed to make her happy.

The foghorn outside wailed mournfully for her lost love.

Chapter Ten

Jamie spent as miserable a weekend as Blythe. He tried everything to distract himself, strenuous exercise, working on briefs he'd brought home from the office, mindless sitcoms on television. Nothing helped. With no one else to talk to, he resorted to carrying on a dialogue with himself.

I suppose you know you made the biggest mistake of your life, he accused himself silently.

"I did it for her sake," Jamie muttered to his mirror image.

Is that the real reason, or could it be that the idea of marriage scares you? his alter ego asked.

"Of course it scares me!" Jamie shouted at the bathroom mirror. "Haven't I seen enough horrible examples!"

Blythe says it doesn't have to be that way, the quiet voice reminded him.

"Because she *wants* to believe that. She doesn't know the time would come when marriage isn't only romance and excitement. That's when boredom sets in."

Honesty made Jamie play the devil's advocate. *For her, or for you?*

He rejected the notion as soon as it surfaced. "Don't be a jackass! I'll love Blythe for the rest of my life."

Then aren't you being a jackass to give her up?

Jamie scowled at himself in the mirror. "It's better than watching her love die. She isn't like my mother. Blythe wouldn't look for somebody new. She'd hang in there and be a dutiful wife, pretending our lovemaking still satisfied her and that she really enjoyed my company. Losing her that way would be more painful than making the break final now."

Could anything be worse than what you're going through?

"I'll get over it." Jamie stalked grimly out of the bedroom.

Jamie had as much trouble buckling down to work on Monday as Blythe did. He, too, intended to skip lunch, but his father dropped in unexpectedly.

Fred wouldn't take no for an answer. "How often do we have an opportunity like this? We haven't spent any time together in a dog's age."

"And nobody else you know is free for lunch," Jamie deduced cynically.

Fred grinned, not bothering to deny the allegation. "Come on, Jamison, don't be a drudge. It isn't a family trait."

"Even so, I'm really swamped today. Perhaps we can have a drink after work."

"Why put off what you can do right now? We'll go to the Stockholder's Club. Ramon makes the only civilized martini in this town."

Jamie gave in because he knew that arguing would be a waste of time. They went to Fred's private club, a prestigious place with leather chairs, hushed conversation and obsequious service. It wouldn't have been Jamie's choice, but after a drink he felt himself relaxing somewhat. He even tried to demonstrate interest in his father's life.

"What have you been doing these last months?" he asked.

"Spending most of my time in Palm Beach. I rented a house there. I'm considering buying it and settling down."

"That doesn't sound like you," Jamie remarked.

Fred smiled. "I meant settling down in the sense of making Florida my home base."

"You really prefer it there?"

"It has a few minor drawbacks, but the advantages make up for it."

Jamie nodded. "I've heard the weather is balmy most of the year."

"I was referring to the women. Palm Beach is a virtual bachelor's paradise. You really must come down and visit me, Jamison."

"Perhaps I will someday," Jamie replied vaguely.

"It's an entirely different way of life. More casual." Fred winked at him. "The girls run around all day in skimpy little bikinis."

Jamie forced a smile. "I see you're still looking."

"Why not? If the good Lord hadn't meant men to enjoy women, he wouldn't have made so many beautiful ones."

"That's one point of view."

"It's the only one. Sex keeps a man young."

"Then you should live forever," Jamie commented sardonically.

"That's a little ambitious. However, with luck, I hope to go with a smile on my face."

"Let's order," Jamie said abruptly. "I have to get back to the office."

He managed to change the subject for a while. They talked about restaurants and luxury vacation spots. Jamie tried to discuss politics, mentioning the pressing issues facing the country, but Fred wasn't interested. While they were having coffee, he gradually returned to his favorite subject.

"You're working too hard, my boy. Frankly you look terrible." Fred's disapproving frown turned into a leer. "Or is it just lack of sleep?"

"A little of both."

"Well, you're young. You can burn the candle at both ends. I must admit I can't perform like I used to."

"That's hard to believe," Jamie remarked ironically.

"Appearances are deceiving. I'm holding up rather well, though, don't you think?" Fred smoothed his hair carefully. "My barber uses a new product. It covers the gray without giving that obviously dyed appearance. Looks natural, doesn't it?"

"Why do you bother?"

"Because I don't want to look like an old geezer when I'm out with a young girl. Chaps like that are pathetic."

"Have you ever considered dating women your own age?" Jamie asked evenly.

"Surely you're joking! What do you think keeps me young? I'm living every man's fantasy."

"Not *every* man's."

"Meaning yourself? Don't be a hypocrite, Jamison. You can't tell me you practice celibacy."

"I don't consider myself promiscuous," Jamie answered austerely.

"If you're not taking advantage of your opportunities, then you're a fool. When I was your age—well, never mind that," Fred said hastily.

"When you were my age you were married, but that didn't slow you down."

Fred looked uncomfortable for the first time. "So you knew about that."

"Everybody did, except possibly the gardener. Couldn't you at least have been more circumspect?"

"I suppose I could have exercised more discretion," Fred conceded. "But I fulfilled my marital obligations. Your mother had nothing to complain about. She was doing what she wanted, and so was I."

"That's not a marriage, it's a legal agreement!"

"What on earth do you think marriage is, my boy?" Fred asked in amusement.

Jamie's flash of anger subsided. "I grew up holding that view," he said slowly.

"It's too bad more people aren't as realistic."

"Realism is no guarantee of permanence, evidently," Jamie observed.

"Everything wears out sooner or later. Marriage is no exception. The entire concept is flawed to begin with. It's unnatural to expect a man to be faithful to one woman all his life."

Jamie stared at him with a kind of morbid curiosity. "Haven't you ever met a woman who was everything you were looking for? Someone you wanted to be with, day and night?"

"I've known a multitude of women like that." Fred laughed. "Fortunately the feeling wears off. Usually when I meet someone younger and prettier. I detest using a cliché, but variety *is* the spice of life. I'm sure you've found that out for yourself."

"No. I'm not like you."

"Really? Then why aren't *you* married? I couldn't help noticing you were quite taken with that pretty girl at your apartment the other day. But you don't intend to marry her, do you?''

Jamie gazed at his father wordlessly, as though he'd never seen him before.

"Whether you think so or not, you're exactly like me," Fred continued. "We both know marriage is a not-so-tender trap. Luckily you learned by my example."

"You're right," Jamie said quietly. "It took me a long time, but I did." He shoved his chair back abruptly. "I have to go."

"I haven't finished my coffee yet," Fred complained. "What's the big hurry?"

"I have to do something I should have done a long time ago."

Jamie felt as if blinders had been removed from his eyes. Today he saw his father for what he was, an insecure man who measured his worth by the number of women he could bed down. Certainly he'd never accomplished anything else in his life. Or ever tried to.

No wonder his wife grew bored with him. If she *had* ever tried to make the marriage work, he hadn't met her halfway. He was probably even a lousy lover. Selfish men usually were.

In spite of Jamie's discovery of just how superficial his father was, he couldn't help feeling sorry for the man. Fred didn't realize what a pathetic figure he was, working frantically to stave off the aging process, chasing young girls who went out with him because of his money and influence and probably laughed at him behind his back. What a sad future he had. In the end he'd be alone, with no one to love him, because he'd never loved anyone himself. The thought was chilling.

Jamie finally realized how warped his own views were because of him. Except for this last-minute reprieve, that could be his own future. But he wasn't like his father in any way. He hadn't even had much contact with him, actually. None of his father's traits had rubbed off on him, only a horrible misconception that almost ruined his life. Blythe had been right all along. A marriage *could* succeed if both partners wanted it to.

If only it wasn't too late! Would Blythe give him another chance? She didn't have any reason to. Most women would slam the door in his face, but Blythe was special. She was sweet and patient and understanding. Lord knows she had to be to put up with him this long! Would she be willing to do it one more time? Jamie swore at the traffic that hemmed him in, prolonging the suspense.

Despite his impatience to get to Blythe, he made one stop first. At Tiffany's. This was another thing he should have done long ago.

Striding into the elegant shop, Jamie told the salesman, "I want the most perfect engagement ring you have."

The transaction took very little time, considering the cost. Jamie selected a large, flawless diamond set with sparkling baguettes. He paid for the ring and put the small velvet box in his pocket, refusing the clerk's offer to gift wrap it.

Jamie clenched the velvet box like a talisman as he entered the advertising agency. At least it would show Blythe that he really had changed. When her office was empty, he looked all around for her, then went back to the receptionist's desk.

"She isn't here," the woman told him.

"I *know* that." Jamie tried to restrain his impatience. "Do you know where she is?"

"I think she left for the day."

"Could you find out?" he grated.

His tone of voice produced an injured look, but the women pushed an intercom button. "Do you know if Blythe is coming back?"

A disembodied voice answered, "I didn't know she was gone. Ask Doug."

Jamie's tension mounted as the woman pressed more buttons and questioned several other people. It seemed like a bad omen. Blythe was lost to him forever.

Finally the receptionist said, "I was right. She won't be back today."

"Did she have an appointment with a client? Do you know where she went?"

"I have no idea."

Jamie left the office and drove to Blythe's house. He didn't telephone first, because what he had to say couldn't be said over the phone. If she wasn't at home, he intended to camp on her doorstep and wait till she returned.

As he rather expected, there was no answer when he rang Blythe's doorbell. She hadn't come home. Unless she'd seen him drive up, and didn't want to talk to him. On the off chance that she was trying to avoid him, he banged loudly on the door and called her name.

"If you're in there, you might as well open up. I'm not leaving."

The door across the hall opened instead, and an older woman peered out a little warily. "Blythe isn't home," she said.

"What time does she usually get here?"

"Different times, but she won't be back for a few days. She asked me to water her plants while she's gone."

"Where did she go?" This was one setback Jamie hadn't anticipated.

"I couldn't tell you. She just said she was taking a few days off. I told her to have a good time, and I'd look after things here," the neighbor said. "We do that for each other."

Jamie's frustration rose to epic proportions during the woman's long-winded answer. "Surely you must have some idea where she went."

"No. She didn't say, and I didn't ask her. I don't pry into other people's affairs."

Jamie took a deep breath. "I understand, but it's terribly important that I get in touch with Blythe immediately. Did she give you a number where she could be reached in case of emergency? I'd appreciate any information you can give me."

The older woman was impressed by his haggard appearance. "I can't tell you any more than I already have, but her sister would know where Blythe is."

"Claire!" Jamie exclaimed. "Of course! Why didn't I think of that?"

"Do you know Claire?" The woman seemed reassured. "She's a lovely person, isn't she? Both of the girls are."

Jamie didn't wait to hear all of her comments. He raced out to his car like a man pursued by demons.

After getting Claire's address from a telephone book in a drugstore phone booth, he drove to Blythe's sister's house, cursing at every red light.

Jenny opened the door. "Who are you?" She looked at him curiously. "Are you selling something?"

Jamie couldn't help smiling. "No, I came to see your mother."

"What's your name?" After he gave it to her, she asked, "Are you Auntie Blythe's friend?"

"I hope so," he answered soberly.

"She doesn't like you anymore."

Jamie sighed. "I was afraid of that."

"Mommy told Daddy she hopes you get your comeuppance one day. What does that mean?"

"It means she doesn't like me, either. I'm not very popular with your family," he said wryly.

"Who are you talking to, Jenny?" Claire called from the kitchen. Her expression changed when she came into the hall and saw for herself. "I didn't expect to see you here," she remarked evenly.

"I came to find out where Blythe is," Jamie answered.

"Is he Auntie Blythe's boyfriend?" Jenny asked.

"We'll talk about it later," Claire told her. "Go in your room and play."

"I don't have anyone to play with."

"Then go watch television."

After the little girl had grumblingly complied, Claire said, "Blythe doesn't want to see you."

"I gathered as much from your daughter. She's quite direct." Jamie smiled appealingly.

Claire didn't return his smile. "Then believe her. You're wasting your time."

"I don't blame you for detesting me. I treated Blythe badly, but I hope to make it up to her."

"*She* bought that line, but *I* don't," Claire said tersely.

"May I just come in and talk to you?" Jamie pleaded.

After a moment's hesitation Claire grudgingly opened the door wider, then led the way to the kitchen.

Folding her arms, she leaned against the sink and looked at him unemotionally. "Okay, talk."

"First, I want to apologize for all the pain I've caused."

"That doesn't make up for anything. You don't realize how miserable you made her. Blythe really loved you."

"I hope she still does."

"She'll get over it. All she needs is a little time."

"I want to marry her," Jamie said quietly.

"You expect me to believe that?" Claire looked at him in disgust. "You've been running like a scared rabbit just to avoid doing that very thing."

"I freely admit I was a fool."

"*I* could have told you that. You don't deserve a fantastic girl like Blythe."

"I admit that, too. But I love her."

"When did you discover this amazing fact? The last I heard, you told her to go out and find someone else. Well, thank heaven, this time Blythe took you at your word."

"I wasn't thinking straight that night."

"A lot of good that does! Do you know how much thought she put into that party?" Claire demanded. "Not to trap you into something you didn't want to do. To let you see for yourself the affection that couples can feel for each other. She was always saying, 'Poor Jamie, nobody loves him.'" Claire mimicked her sister mockingly. "Well, I can see why. Because you don't know the meaning of the word. You have to give to get."

"I'm thirty-four years old, and I only found that out this afternoon."

She looked at him suspiciously. "Who showed you the light?"

"Let's just say I got all the wrong signals from authority figures."

"I know about your parents' divorce. That doesn't mean the same thing has to happen to you. You're a different person than your father, and Blythe isn't like your mother."

"You couldn't be more right," Jamie answered fervently. "And I'm prepared to spend the rest of my life making up for the pain I've inflicted."

Claire was impressed in spite of herself, yet she was afraid to trust him. "How do I know you won't feel threatened again and walk out on her still another time?"

He took the velvet box out of his pocket and opened it. "I went to her office today to give her this."

Claire stared at it and whistled. "I will say when you apologize, you go all out."

"I hope she'll accept it," Jamie answered simply. "Will you tell me where she is?"

Claire looked troubled. "Maybe you'd better sit down. I'll pour us some coffee."

He didn't want any, but he did as she said. Claire held his future in her hands.

She sat down facing him. "I believe everything you've said—up to a point. You and Blythe have something powerful between you. I don't know if it's love or merely sex, but whatever it is, it's pretty awesome. She's utterly hooked on you, and from the looks of you tonight, you're a basket case without her."

"Doesn't that tell you we belong together? What's bothering you?"

"I just have to be sure of your motives. I wonder if you're willing to take the big step because this time you pushed Blythe too far and you know it's the only way you can get her back. A coerced marriage doesn't stand a chance."

"I don't know how to convince you," Jamie said helplessly. "I'd like to marry Blythe tomorrow, but I'm willing to wait if she shares your doubts. All I ask is a chance to prove my love. I've told her, now I'm prepared to show her."

Claire stared into his eyes for a long moment, then she smiled. "Welcome to the family, Jamie."

His voice was thick with emotion. "I'll be the best damn brother-in-law you ever had."

"You'd better be, since you're the only one I ever expect to have." She used a light tone to cover her own emotion.

"I guarantee it! Now tell me where she is."

"At our house in Stinson Beach. You can use the phone in the den. I'll give you the number."

"No way." Jamie grinned. "This calls for the personal touch."

"I get your point. But it seems a shame for the poor kid to spend another miserable night. Make sure you start out early in the morning."

"You don't honestly think I'm going to wait until tomorrow?"

"That road is dangerous at night, Jamie, especially if there's fog."

"I've hit bottom and bounced back. Nothing can happen to me," he said confidently.

Claire could see it was useless to argue. "Just promise to take it easy on the curves. If you kill yourself, Blythe will never forgive me."

Jamie kissed her cheek. "Don't worry, I have too much at stake to get careless now."

The fire had an hypnotic effect on Blythe. Her eyelids drooped and she dozed off. When the doorbell awakened her, she groaned. It could only be the Halsteads, checking to see if she needed anything. They meant well, but they'd interrupted the first rest she'd had in days.

Blythe went to the door, trying to look pleased to see them. The unexpected sight of Jamie froze her to the spot.

They stared at each other wordlessly, both gripped by powerful emotions. After never expecting to see him again, this seemed like a miracle. Blythe didn't even notice the weary lines on his face. To her, he was the answer to a prayer.

It took great effort to remind herself that this dream was really a nightmare. Jamie brought only pain. "What are you doing here?" she whispered.

"Did you honestly think I could stay away?"

She turned aside. "We said our goodbyes."

He followed her into the living room and closed the door. "I thought we had. I've been going through hell."

"I'm surprised I didn't see you there," she answered bitterly.

"I know it's been hard on you, too, darling. I've made a grand mess of everything."

"It doesn't matter any longer."

"You can't really mean that. We have to talk, Blythe."

"Our last talk said it all. You presented a very convincing case."

Jamie tried to smile. "I've uncovered new evidence."

"Aren't you a little confused? You won, remember?"

"How could I possibly win if I lost you?"

Blythe steeled herself against the naked hunger in his eyes. "I won't let you do this to me again, Jamie. I always hope things will turn out differently, but they never do."

"I don't blame you for not trusting me. All I can say in my own defense is that I never meant to hurt you. That was the reason I backed off so many times."

"If you really cared about me, you'd leave me alone. Are you trying to discover my breaking point? Well, I've just about reached it." Her strain was indeed evident. Every instinct was urging her to throw herself into his arms and believe all his lies.

"I want to marry you, Blythe," he said quietly.

That one was too much to swallow! "You asked me once before—with the same degree of ardor," she said mockingly. "When's the wedding date, the middle of never?"

"I'd like it to be tomorrow, if it's at all possible."

His answer startled Blythe, along with the sincerity in his voice. She wavered between suspicion and joy. Suspicion won out. She'd been burned too often.

"No. Claire warned me against something like this. I promised her I wouldn't let you do it to me again."

"If it's any inducement, we have your sister's blessing."

"I'll bet! You weren't high on her list to begin with. Now she wouldn't trust you to pet her dog."

"Tell me!" A smile relieved some of the strain on Jamie's face. "She didn't even want to let me in the house."

"That sounds more like Claire. *I* might be gullible where you're concerned, but your glib speeches would never work on her."

"How do you think I knew where you were?"

"Claire wouldn't tell you," Blythe said uncertainly.

"Nothing could have kept me away, sweetheart, but I'm not Sherlock Holmes. It would have taken me a while to find out."

"What could you possibly have said to convince her?" Blythe asked in amazement.

"It wasn't easy," Jamie replied ruefully. "Even after I showed her this." He took the blue velvet box out of his pocket and handed it to her.

She opened it gingerly, as though expecting something to pop out. When she saw the sparkling diamond, her eyes widened. "It's beautiful!"

"Not nearly as lovely as you," he answered huskily. "Nothing could be."

"I don't understand," Blythe said helplessly. "Only last Friday night we agreed not to see each other again. It was your idea."

"I can't believe I was too stupid to realize you were right and I was wrong."

"What changed your mind?" The ring would seem to be proof, but what explanation could there be?

"I had lunch with my father today." Jamie's face set in the austere lines Blythe was all too familiar with.

"Seeing your parents usually reminds you of why marriage doesn't work."

"It's ironic that I would pick a loser as a role model. My father has never excelled at anything."

"Most people would consider him very successful," she had to point out.

"Let me tell you what I discovered today."

Blythe didn't resist when Jamie led her to the couch. She listened intently as he told her about the lunch with his father and the revelation he'd had.

"Children can't help being influenced by their parents, and I was no exception," he concluded. "They never told me a relationship between a man and a woman could be full and enriching, because they never discovered it for themselves. I feel very sorry for them."

"So do I," Blythe murmured.

"But all this time I've been unconsciously repeating their mistakes. It wasn't until I took a good look at my father today that I could see where I was headed."

Blythe's dawning happiness dimmed. "You came back because you don't want to wind up alone like him?"

"No, darling. I came back because I've finally become the man you thought you were in love with. The one who wants a home and children, but most of all, the wife he's always dreamed about. Will you take me back, Blythe?"

Tears blurred her vision as she threw her arms around his neck. "Welcome home, Jamie."

They clung together with the desperation of lovers who had been separated for years instead of days. Uttering broken endearments, Jamie strewed feverish kisses over her neck, her cheeks, her closed eyelids.

Blythe whispered her own words of love while she tangled her fingers tightly in his hair. She had to hold on to him to reassure herself. Pulling his head down, she captured his mouth for a kiss that satisfied all her pent-up longing.

Jamie strained her so close that she could feel his heart beating wildly, in time with her own. They caressed each other frantically, showing their love in a way that words couldn't express.

Finally the wild momentum slowed and their taut bodies relaxed. Jamie's desperate embrace loosened, and he stroked Blythe's hair gently. She nestled in his arms, filled with the wonder of their love.

"It scares me to think of how close I came to losing you," he said soberly.

Blythe kissed his throat. "Let's not think about it anymore."

"I can't help myself. It was such a close call. If my father hadn't insisted that I have lunch with him, we wouldn't be together like this." Jamie's voice held wonder. "It's frightening to think that our entire future was changed because of a whim of his."

She smiled. "Do you really think that's what it was?"

"What else could it be? He just happened to be at loose ends and decided to pick me to fill the gap. That's what makes it such a miracle. Dad and I never spent any time together before."

"You can call it a miracle, I call it destiny. Ours was written in the stars long ago."

"I'm beginning to think you're right. I only wish I'd trusted in them sooner," Jamie said wryly. "It would have saved me a lot of suffering."

"I'll make you forget it," Blythe murmured.

He gazed at her adoringly. "You already have, my love."

* * * * *

LOVE AND
LOVE AND THE LIBRA MAN...

by Wendy Corsi Staub

In October the world is at its most dazzling, and Halloween caps off the month with a festive air. The Libra man loves to entertain, and he'll delight in planning the ultimate Halloween masquerade party! Born under the sign of justice, he'll don black robes, borrow a gavel and go as a judge. This charming gentleman is sure to be a gracious host—especially to that certain female guest who's lucky enough to capture his attention!

In Tracy Sinclair's *Anything But Marriage,* Libra man Jamison Marshall clashes with fellow Libra Blythe Reynolds over a valuable painting, but their story has a harmonious ending. On Halloween she'll be sure to make him smile and reminisce when she shows up at the party wearing a smock and beret, posing as an artist!

Which costume would the Libra man expect YOU to wear to his gala event?

The *Aries* woman is as ambitious as they come, and she has boundless energy to accomplish her lofty goals. Since 1992 is an Olympic year, she'll put on her best workout clothes, hang a heavy medallion around her neck and go as a gold medalist. After all, she won't settle for less than the best . . . which must be why she's so smitten by the Libra man!

The *Taurus* woman often skips meals and goes straight for the dessert—she has an insatiable sweet tooth! On Halloween she'll have lots of fun concocting a costume that reflects her favorite indulgence—an ice-cream sundae, complete with a big cardboard "spoon" and a papier-mâché "cherry!" The Libra man is sure to find her irresistible!

The intellectual *Gemini* woman has always admired history's great philosophers—here's her chance to impersonate one! In a white tunic and sandals, she'll come disguised as Socrates and will captivate guests with her clever, logical observations. The Libra man is sure to take opposing views just to keep things lively—and fair—and the two of them will debate enthusiastically for hours!

The domestic *Cancer* woman enjoys whipping up yummy desserts as a hobby, so when Halloween rolls around, she'll dress up as a pastry chef! Wearing a frilly apron and wielding a rolling pin, she'll make guests' mouths water when she describes her next culinary creation. The Libra man might pretend to find a smudge of flour on her cheek . . . and steal a kiss when he wipes it away!

Who can that be, flashing a flirtatious smile behind those whiskers and twirling her "tail" in a "come hither" manner? Why, the adorable *Leo* woman, of course! The Libra man will discover that she may be the life of the party, but later she'll be *purr*fectly content to curl up alone with him

The *Virgo* woman is just an old-fashioned girl at heart, and she'll indulge her fondest fantasies when she dresses as one on Halloween. From her ladylike bonnet to the tips of her high-button boots, she'll be sweetly feminine . . . and when she drops her handkerchief, the gallant Libra man will come running!

The mystical *Scorpio* woman loves spooky Halloween, and she'll be the hit of the party as an exotic gypsy fortune-teller. Lots of jangling, dangling earrings and bracelets and a long flowing skirt will enhance her authenticity when she offers to read palms, and the Libra man will be her first volunteer. She'll see that he has a long "love" line—but *he* might just tell *her* a thing or two about *their* future . . . together!

The archer is the *Sagittarius* woman's symbol, and she'll use that as an inspiration for her Halloween costume: Robin Hood! In green tights and a brown tunic, she'll do the legend justice, but another famous archer—Cupid—might put in an appearance when the Libra man introduces himself to the Sagittarius woman!

The traditional *Capricorn* woman tends toward the conventional in most matters, and Halloween costumes aren't an exception. Her pointy black hat and long black cape are a classic party disguise that will certainly keep the Libra man spellbound! And at midnight she'll hop on her magic broomstick and whisk him away!

The free-spirited *Aquarius* woman is a true flower child at heart, and Halloween is her opportunity to dress the part. In a tie-dye T-shirt, love beads and a big floppy hat, she'll be the ultimate "hippy." Since "peace" is something she

and the Libra man both value, they're sure to get along fa-
mously!

The romantic *Pisces* woman sometimes wishes life was like
a fairy tale, and on Halloween she'll play make-believe just
for a night. Yards of tulle and a rhinestone tiara will trans-
form her into a sparkling fairy princess, and when she waves
her magic wand, her prince will miraculously appear—in the
form of a handsome Libra man!

HE'S MORE THAN A MAN, HE'S ONE OF OUR

Dear Christina,

Stationed here in the Gulf, as part of the peacekeeping effort, I've learned that family and children are the most important things about life. I need a woman who wants a family as much as I do....

Love, Joe

Dear Joe,

How can I tell you this...?

Love, Christina

Dear Reader,
Read between the lines as Toni Collins's FABULOUS FATHER, Joe Parish, and Christina Holland fall in love through the mail in LETTERS FROM HOME. Coming this October from

Silhouette
R O M A N C E™

FFATHER2

Silhouette
R O M A N C E™

═══ HEARTLAND ═══
HOLIDAYS

Christmas bells turn into wedding bells for the Gallagher siblings in Stella Bagwell's *Heartland Holidays* trilogy.

THEIR FIRST THANKSGIVING (#903) in November
Olivia Westcott had once rejected Sam Gallagher's proposal—
and in his stubborn pride, he'd refused to hear her reasons why.
Now Olivia is back...and it is about time Sam Gallagher listened!

THE BEST CHRISTMAS EVER (#909) in December
Soldier Nick Gallagher had come home to be the best man at his
brother's wedding—not to be a groom! But when he met single
mother Allison Lee, he knew he'd found his bride.

NEW YEAR'S BABY (#915) in January
Kathleen Gallagher had given up on love and marriage until she
came to the rescue of neighbor Ross Douglas . . . and the newborn
baby he'd found on his doorstep!

Come celebrate the holidays with Silhouette Romance!

TAKE A WALK ON THE DARK SIDE OF LOVE

October is the shivery season, when chill winds blow and shadows walk the night. Come along with us into a haunting world where love and danger go hand in hand, where passions will thrill you and dangers will chill you. Come with us to

In this newest short story collection from Silhouette Books, three of your favorite authors tell tales just perfect for a spooky autumn night. Let Anne Stuart introduce you to "The Monster in the Closet," Helen R. Myers bewitch you with "Seawitch," and Heather Graham Pozzessere entice you with "Wilde Imaginings."

Silhouette Shadows™
Haunting a store near you this October.

Take 4 bestselling love stories FREE

Plus get a FREE surprise gift!

FEB 22 1994   NOV 2 1993

Silhouette
R O M A N C E ™